Cathy Hopkins

Million Dollar Mates

Golden Girl

SIMON

First published in Great Britain in 2012 by Simon and Schuster UK Ltd
A CBS COMPANY

Simon & Schuster UK Ltd
1st Floor,
222 Gray's Inn Road,
London WC1X 8HB

A CIP catalogue record for this book
is available from the British Library.

PB ISBN: 978-1-84738-760-8
E-BOOK ISBN: 978-1-84738-995-4

1 3 5 7 9 10 8 6 4 2

Printed and bound by CPI Group (UK) Ltd, Croydon, CR0 4YY

www.simonandschuster.co.uk
www.cathyhopkins.com

1

Easter Hols

'It's time for some serious study,' said Mrs Moran, my English teacher, before she dismissed class for Easter. 'You all have to get your heads down this holiday.'

'No late nights,' Dad said when I got home from school. 'If you're to get good grades in your GCSEs, you have to focus.'

'Time-manage your studying,' said Aunt Maddie when she dropped by as we were having supper. It was macaroni cheese, one of my faves. 'Break it down into do-able chunks. Oh, and we need to have a long talk soon about the subjects you want to do for A-level.'

'You need fish oils,' Gran said, when she called later the same evening. 'They're good for the brain.'

What planet are they all on? Planet B-4-Boring, that's what. I'm so not looking forward to the holidays. Not that I don't take my schoolwork seriously, I do, but I take having fun seriously too.

'Study, study, study. What subjects are you going to do in Sixth Form? What do you think you might like to do when you leave school?' I said to my mate Pia, when she came to sleep over. 'That's all I hear lately. And *fish oils*? Doesn't anyone realise it's spring? The daffodils are out. The skies are clear. Birds are singing. The nights are getting longer and I, Jess Hall, have a boyfriend!'

I do too. A proper one. My first, even though I'm fifteen. I've not had a lot of luck with boys up until now. But all that's changed. It's finally happened. He's not someone I have a crush on from afar who hardly notices me. Or someone who likes me but won't commit and messes with my head (like Tom Robertson – he's so last term). No. I'm having a *relationship*. Dates, texts, holding hands, listening to music curled up on the sofa, snog sessions . . . something I have to say he's very good at. And it all feels absolutely blooming lovely.

His name is JJ Lewis. We're JJ and Jess. Jess and JJ.

Pia got into her blue-and-white striped nightie, sat on the end of my bed and began to apply apple-scented body lotion to her legs. 'My mum's just the same,' she said. 'Nag, nag, nag. Like, I don't *know* what I want to do when I leave school. I keep changing my mind.'

'Me too! Art? English? I have no idea,' I said as I got into my nightie, which is like Pia's, only pink and white. We got them in the sale at Westfield shopping mall after Christmas.

'It's not as if we want to be strippers, for goodness' sake,' said Pia. 'Now that really *would* give them something to talk about!' She got up and began to shimmy around my bedroom.

I laughed and looked at my reflection in the mirror. A tall, slim girl with shoulder-length chestnut-coloured hair and big blue eyes looked back. 'Hey, you. What do you want to be?' I asked myself. 'Come on, girl. Make up your mind!'

Pia came to stand next to me. At five foot three, she only just comes up to my shoulder but I never think of her as small. She's a curvy cherub with a big, *big* personality.

'Look at us. Here we are in Year Eleven, both

fifteen,' she said as she slicked back her short, dark hair, 'and I wonder who we'll be in five years – or even ten. What will we look like then, I wonder? Will we be lawyers? Doctors? Dancers? Teachers?'

'Mates,' I said. 'We can be sure of that much.'

Pia nodded. 'For life.' She knelt down on the floor and got into the sleeping bag I'd laid out for her earlier on top of the roll-out mattress beside my bed.

'I was thinking I might like to work in a cats and dogs rescue home,' I said as I looked over at my cat, Dave, who had settled himself for the night as he always did – a mass of black-and-white fur at the foot of my bed.

Pia shook her head. 'You wouldn't last a week, Jess – you'd get too upset. People take their pets to those places when the animals get ill or old. You'd bring them all home with you and have to hide them in your wardrobe. Probably doesn't pay much, either. So it depends on whether you want to be rich.'

'I want to do something that pays well, course I do. Who doesn't? But I don't know *what*. In the meantime, all anyone goes on about is studying, subject choices and careers.'

'I've tried telling Mum that life has to be all about balance but she's a workaholic, just like your dad.'

'They ought to get married,' I said.

'Yeah, right. They'd kill each other. I don't know which of them is the bigger control-freak.'

Pia and I live next door to each other in the staff area at Number 1, Porchester Park. My dad's the general manager and Pia's mum runs the spa and there's a mews house on site for each of our families that comes with the job. They're pretty ordinary houses with small box rooms, built for the staff who have to be there twenty-four seven to cater for the every need of the people who live in the main apartment block. Lots of the residents have their own private live-in staff too: chefs, chauffeurs, minders, masseurs, housekeepers, PAs and so on but there's also a fleet of staff that comes with the place to provide whatever else they might want – be it a limo, the latest designer dresses brought in for a bit of home-shopping, or a cheese-and-tomato sandwich at midnight. Porchester Park is the most luxurious, prestigious address in London and its residents are the super rich and the international elite – A-list actors, businessmen, some royals, celebs or just plain old billionaires. Dad's job is to keep things running smoothly and ensure that what a resident wants, a resident gets.

I sat on my bed and began to apply my aloe vera

moisturiser. 'Let's forget about school for a bit. For this evening, anyway. Let's talk about more important stuff. Like, what do you think is the secret of a good relationship? Do you think opposites attract and that's the best combination? Or do you think you need to share your views on everything? Or can that get boring? And how do you keep a boy interested in you after the first few dates?' I needed to know all this stuff, being a relationship newbie. I wanted it to work with me and JJ.

Pia snuggled down into her sleeping bag. I love these late night chats with her when it's just girlie time and we can talk about anything and everything, from boys, friends and school to what we want to do with our lives, our fave beauty products (lately we're taking moisturising *very* seriously) to deep stuff like whether there's a God or not. Pia's more of a boy expert than I am. She's had three relationships so far and is now dating the lovely, handsome Henry, who also lives in the staff area. His dad looks after the underground car park and the fleets of limos and cars that belong to the richies.

Pia considered my question. 'A bit of both, I think,' she said. 'Like, if you're total opposites, you might end up arguing all the time, but if you're very similar, then it can be a bit blah and dull like cottage cheese and you won't learn anything. No fire, spice or challenge. With Henry, we both like a laugh and are chilled about most things, but he's a total music and movie geek, which I'm not. But he gets me into loads of stuff I wouldn't have thought of listening to or going to see, and I end up loving it.'

I felt like I was on a huge learning curve now that JJ and I were dating. Up until now, my love life had consisted of a few flirtations that had come to nothing and trying to find a boy I liked who wasn't into messing around and just seeing how many girls he could get off with (like Tom). 'I want to make it last with JJ and I think I can learn a lot from him,' I said, 'and him from me, because our worlds are totally different . . . but I hope that won't cause problems.'

'Why should it?'

'Duh. He's the son of one of the most famous actors on the planet and I'm Jess Nobody.' JJ is Jefferson Lewis's son and he lives in one of the apartments at Porchester Park. He travels by limo, while I go by tube, bus and foot. He holidays in far-off exotic locations, staying in private villas or five-star hotels. I'm lucky if I get a weekend away in

Bournemouth with Dad's younger brother and his family, where I have to sleep on a pull-out sofabed in the study. JJ's home-schooled, while I go to the local state. He dresses in top designers like Ralph Lauren, Armani and Tommy Hilfiger, while I can barely afford Topshop in the sale. Basically, his family is loaded, and my dad can only just about manage to pay for items on my brother Charlie's and my school list, never mind extras. So, basically, although we live within a few metres of each other, we're worlds apart.

'You're not Jess Nobody. You shouldn't talk yourself down like that. And anyway, the fact that he picked you when he could have gone out with someone from his world means he likes *you*, not what your family do or how much your dad earns.'

'I guess, though I do feel bad when he wants to go somewhere and I can't afford it. But we do agree on loads of stuff, like we've both said that we don't want to play games in our relationship. It's so nice not to think that I have to act cool or keep my feelings to myself.'

'Early days,' said Pia. 'Sometimes you do. I don't think boys like it if you go on about having PMT or how insecure you're feeling about your looks or something – which is why I don't think you should call yourself Jess Nobody. If you really think that, he'll pick up on it. Boys like confidence.'

'Yeah, but I don't want to put on an act.'

'No, I know, I just think you should be yourself right from the beginning. Some girls put on an act when they first start going out with a boy, pretending to always be in a good mood, or always finding his rubbish jokes funny, basically doing whatever he wants to do and going wherever he wants to go, like they're some kind of perfect girl. Then weeks down the line, they can't keep it up and the boy can't make out why they've changed.'

'It's complicated,' I sighed. 'And what you're saying is contradictory. Don't put on an act but don't let him know if I'm feeling insecure? Which is it?'

Pia grinned. 'Both. You'll get the hang of it.'

My phone bleeped that I had a text.

Need 2 C U. Urgent. JJ.

It was eleven o'clock at night. Dad was downstairs. No way would I be able to creep out without him seeing me. I texted back: Am in pjs having sleepover with Pia. Dad on sentry duty downstairs. I cd b shot if I try to leave. Can it wait til a.m.? Is problem?

He texted back. I didn't mean now. No prob. I have

a plan for Easter. Surprise. Hope U like. CU tmoro at 9. My place. JJ XXX

I texted back. XXX ☺

God, life was good – even if I did have to do some studying and swallow some fish oils along the way.

2

Invite

I got up early the next morning, even though it was a Saturday. I needed time to prepare to see JJ. I showered, washed my hair and tried on everything in my wardrobe while Pia snored away on the floor. That girl can sleep through anything. I wanted to look my best but also not appear to be trying too hard. I settled for my skinny jeans, a red top and my red Converse. A touch of make-up and a squirt of the Chanel no 19 that Gran had given me at Christmas and I was ready. I was looking forward to seeing JJ and talking through our plans for the holidays. It was going to be his seventeenth birthday soon. I wanted to quiz JJ's sister, Alisha, about what he might like as a present. What to buy the boy who has everything? I also wanted to take him somewhere special, which was a challenge considering some of the places he must have been in his life. I'd made out a list of things that we could maybe do if he liked the sound of them. I checked it over as I had a quick cup of green tea. Bleurgh. It tasted like boiled grass but, along with the daily moisturising, it was all part of my and Pia's new health and beauty routine.

The list:

A movie.
There were a few new ones opening in Leicester Square but that might be dull for him as he gets to go to all the premieres with his dad and all the stars. I crossed that off.

Greenwich.
He'd never been to Greenwich on the boat down the Thames, so I could take him there. It's like visiting a whole new country and there are loads of shops and stalls to browse plus the park with the Royal Observatory at the top which is the home of

Greenwich meantime and the biggest telescope in England. I ticked that one. I thought he might like that.

Covent Garden.
We could go to watch the street performers then head down to the river to sit at one of the cafés and watch the world go by. I ticked that one too.

Various museums, churches and art galleries.
Could be fun but would be heaving with people, seeing as it was Easter.

Swimming in the ponds at Hampstead Heath.
Again, might be busy but worth considering. JJ and I are both big swimmers and swimming outdoors together would be different.

Richmond Park for a picnic.
I ticked that one.

All these places could be fab except for the fact that JJ might not be allowed to go without Vanya, the family minder, in tow. Mr Lewis insisted that he accompany JJ and his sister, Alisha, whenever they went out in public. I made a mental note to try and find out if JJ could escape without Vanya and, if so, where to. So far, on the few dates we'd had, Vanya had come along too. He was very discreet and kept himself at a distance but both of us were aware that he was always there, watching us. Safety and security are very important to the residents at Porchester Park, both in the building and outside. The only real time we'd had alone was at my house or in his apartment and, even then, my family was around at my place and his family and assorted staff were always there at his. We'd been interrupted mid-snog a few times. *Très* embarrassing.

I'd been to all the locations on the list with Charlie or Pia, but I hoped that it would be different, more romantic, going to them with a boyfriend. I also wanted to get to know JJ better. Because we'd had so little time on our own to talk, I didn't feel that I'd got to know the real boy behind the charming, very polite manner he had. I wanted to know what he thought about all sorts of things, what he wanted to do after college – I think he'd mentioned something about being a lawyer once, but I wasn't sure. I wanted to know what made him laugh, what made him cry. Maybe I'd give him a questionnaire as a joke. It was really hard to find out stuff like that when I was constantly surrounded by my friends. Not that I wanted to shut my mates out. No way. I know the rule. You don't drop mates for a boy. All the same, there has to be some private boy/girl time if we're going to make it work.

At ten to nine, I checked in on a still sleeping Pia, decided to leave her there and set off for the Lewises' apartment.

I stopped at the door that opened into reception from the staff area so that the cameras could read my irises. The security at the block was very high. It was designed by the SAS and all the apartments had bullet-and-bomb-proof windows, plus most of them had panic rooms. It felt cool that I could cruise my way in like this, but then all the staff know who I am and that I'm no threat to anyone. The doors swung open to let me through and I waved to the receptionist, Grace. I noticed she'd had her blonde hair cut into a neat bob. She gave me the briefest of nods as she spritzed water onto an elegant display of bamboo and white orchids in a vase to the right of her desk. Out front, through the floor-to-ceiling glass window, I could see Didier, the doorman and security guard. He glanced over but then turned away to open the door of a sleek black Mercedes that had just driven up. When he isn't busy, he's much friendlier than Grace. She's cold and business-like and saves her smiles for the residents. Yoram, the other security guard, is the same. He doesn't do chit-chat. No-one questions me going upstairs any more, even though, generally, staff don't mix socially with residents. However, everyone who works here knows that I'm mates not only with JJ, but also with Alisha. I often go up to see her or she comes down to hang out with me and Pia. Most of the teens at Porchester Park stay in their exclusive little world, not going out without minders and not mixing with the other teens in the block, never mind the sons and daughters of staff. JJ and Alisha are the exceptions – and Alexei, a Russian boy who arrived just after Christmas. They're all home-schooled and are glad to meet people their own age. Life can be lonely for them up there in their beautiful homes and the one thing that their parents' money hasn't been able to buy them so far is true mates.

None of the staff know that I'm dating JJ, apart from Dad, of course. He doesn't totally approve but he can't object, not with his mantra that what a resident wants, a resident gets. I just don't think he ever expected that a resident would want to date his daughter. It's a mad world and sometimes feels like 'us and them', upstairs-downstairs, but I'm getting used to it and finding out that the residents are not so different, just because they're loaded. They might dress in expensive clothes but inside their feelings are the same. Alisha's the same age as I am and she's never had a proper boyfriend either. She says it's because, for the last few years, her family haven't stayed in one place long enough for her to get into a relationship but I think that it's also because, despite the luxury lifestyle, she doesn't get to meet a lot of boys our age.

Over in a corner, one of the housekeeping staff was changing a candle. They're burnt every day in reception to give the lovely smell that always permeates the building. One day, Pia and I looked up on the internet how much those candles cost. One hundred and twenty pounds, just for one big one! Only the best for Porchester Park residents ... My Aunt Maddie says they have money to burn. She's right there. Pia and I say it's like stepping into Wonderland when we go into the main block. It's another world where no expense is spared and although the public areas are neutral in décor, I've seen inside some of the apartments and know what treasures lie behind those closed doors. Each one is different, depending on which interior designer did the decoration, but there are rare antiques and artefacts, original paintings by the grand masters, priceless Persian rugs, gold-leafed ceilings, state-of-the-art kitchens, bathrooms with marble from France and Italy, and vast living rooms as big as football pitches, most with stunning views through floor-to-ceiling glass windows that look out over the park. One apartment had the whole interior of a French château transported over and incorporated into its rooms, though most apartments tend to favour a more modern, uncluttered look, with everything brand new and the best that money can buy.

'Where are you off to?' asked Dad, suddenly appearing behind me. He was immaculately dressed, as always, in a dark suit and tie and, even though he's my dad, I had to admit he looked handsome, if a little tired. He had shadows under his blue eyes and there were a few grey hairs starting to appear in his mane of dark hair.

I pointed upstairs. 'Er . . . JJ,' I stuttered.

Dad frowned. 'Don't be long up there. I don't mean to be a killjoy but you know what your priority has to be this holiday and it's not boys.'

'I'll be quick,' I promised. 'He . . . he just wanted to tell me something.'

'There'll be plenty of time for boys once your exams are out the way. In the summer. But right now you have to concentrate on what's important.'

Give me a break, I thought. It's only the first day of the Easter holidays and already he's on my case. Didn't he realise that having my first boyfriend was a big thing in my life? Like, *major?* He probably didn't. My lack of boyfriend had never been a topic of conversation between us. And I *would* study. But I also wanted to enjoy myself some of the time.

'I read in one of my *How to Study* guides that time off is important in order to keep a clear head,' I said. It was worth a try, not that Dad knew the meaning of time off or relaxation. His job was full-on. I rarely saw him in casual clothes or chilling out because he's on call twenty-four seven.

'Yes, but time off when you've done a few hours' work. *Not* time off first thing in the morning before you've even started!'

'Dad, it's Saturday. Some people do have weekends, you know.' I couldn't win. Luckily, Dad's mobile rang and, as he went off to answer it, I headed for the lift. A few minutes later, I was up on the

Lewises' floor and JJ was opening the door for me. I still got a rush whenever I saw him because he's easily one of the best-looking boys I've ever met, with a tall, slim frame, short, dark hair, a divine full mouth and beautiful deep brown eyes. He kissed me lightly on the cheek and I caught his light citrus scent. He always smelt lovely and clean, unlike some of the boys at our school who gave off an aroma of stale biscuits or unwashed socks.

'So, what's the big surprise?' I asked as I followed him through into the kitchen where Alisha was seated at the black-and-pearl granite breakfast bar tucking into croissants with Alexei. He waved hello. It was a shame he and Alisha didn't fancy each other because they made a stunning couple, both tall and slim – Alexei with floppy blond hair, cheekbones to die for and pale blue eyes, and Alisha his opposite – sultry-looking and dark-eyed with long brown hair which, though naturally curly, was professionally blowdried every morning to look glossy and straight. They're both into their designer clothes and accessories too – Alexei even more so than Alisha. He's always flashing a Rolex or Cartier watch or showing off the latest phone or gadget he's got. Not that JJ doesn't have the best, too. He does, but he doesn't show it off like Alexei. Alisha did consider Alexei as a boyfriend, as we all did when he first arrived, but, like me, she didn't feel the magnetic pull of chemistry and settled for just being friends instead.

'Hey, Jess,' she said. 'Have you eaten? This apricot jam is to die for and there's freshly squeezed grape juice.'

'Hey,' I replied and went to sit next to her. 'Love the outfit.' She was wearing a white T-shirt and pink tracksuit bottoms with a white stripe down the side.

'Found me a girlfriend yet?' asked Alexei. I loved hearing him speak. He had a good English accent but there was a hint of Russian on some words. So exotic-sounding. Some girl was going to fall head over heels for him. No question about it.

I laughed and shook my head. 'If you came into school one day, I'd imagine there'd be a line of girls queuing up to be your girlfriend.' Maybe next term I'll start a dating agency, with Alexei as the first to register. Or run a speed-dating event to raise money for a school charity. That would be fun.

At the other end of the bar, JJ busied himself with his laptop as Alisha poured me a glass of juice then handed it to me. I took a sip. It was divine and tasted so different to carton juice. The Lewises are big on fresh juices and everything is organic and prepared by their housekeeper, Marguerite. She even made them jams with apricots and peaches specially flown in from Italy.

'I want you to look at a slideshow,' JJ said. 'I've been working on it all morning.'

'Why not use the cinema room?' Alisha suggested. 'Let her see it all on a larger scale.'

'Good idea. Won't be a mo,' said JJ as he picked up his laptop.

'Can I come and see?' asked Alexei.

'Of course,' said JJ, and he disappeared out of the door.

'So, what's the surprise?' I asked.

'If I told you, I'd have to kill you,' said Alisha. 'But I think you'll like it.'

When Alisha and I first met, we didn't get on: I hated her and thought she was a spoilt princess, while she thought I was a stuck-up pain. As time went on, we got to know each other better and both of us realised that we were unhappy at Porchester Park for similar reasons. Both of us felt displaced and a little lonely and we'd been taking it out on each other. It was funny. I thought she had it all – the designer clothes, a fabulous lifestyle – and she thought *I* had it all because I had freedom and mates whereas she couldn't go anywhere without Vanya watching her every move. Once we realised that we were both unhappy, we started talking and found that we got on and we've been friends ever since. She's also a Sagittarian like me, and too outspoken for her own good, which gets her into trouble sometimes.

'Ready,' called JJ.

Alisha, Alexei and I got off our stools and went to join JJ in the cinema room. Most of the apartments have private cinemas and the Lewises' is no different. Theirs is dark red with black-out blinds and two enormous, soft brown L-shaped leather sofas so that you can sit with your legs out in front of you. Alexei and I flopped back onto one and Alisha took the other.

'Let the show begin!' said Alisha.

At the back of the room, JJ pressed a button on his computer and images of a sunny location started to show on the screen. It looked amazing, wherever it was. A lake with a fairytale white palace in the middle. Mountains in the distance. A vast honey-coloured palace on the lakeshore with balconies looking over the water. Shots of women in saris in bright jewel colours. Carved temples.

'Is it India?' I asked.

'Udaipur in Rajasthan,' said Alexei. '*Ja?*'

'*Ja*. Right,' said JJ.

'We're going for Easter,' said Alisha.

My heart sank as JJ let a few more photos play across the screen and all my plans for the holidays disappeared into nothing. JJ would be on the other side of the world in the glorious location up on the screen and I'd be chained to my desk surrounded by school books with nothing but a list of places we could have gone to screwed up in the bin. Bummer.

JJ pressed a button for the slides to finish and came to sit on the sofa with me. 'Dad's been shooting some scenes there for his latest movie.'

I didn't want him to see how disappointed I was so I made myself smile. 'It looks beautiful, stunning,' I said. 'You'll have a wonderful time.'

'I think it will be perfect timing to go to India,' said Alisha, 'seeing as I'm going through an existential crisis.'

'I thought that was something that happened when you're middle-aged. You're only fifteen,' I said. 'What is it exactly, anyway?'

Alisha did her tragic look – one that I have to say she does very well. 'It can happen at any age. It's a sense of feeling alone in the world, thinking about the big stuff like the meaning of life.'

'In that case, I'm having one too,' I said. 'I'm always thinking about stuff like that.'

'And I, being Russian, 'ave these things in my blood,' said Alexei.

'The meaning of life is forty-two,' said JJ.

I laughed. I knew he was referring to a book I'd read called *The Hitchhiker's Guide to the Galaxy*, where it says the answer to the meaning of life is forty-two. It made me laugh because I thought, why not? It's as good an answer as any.

'You're mad,' said Alisha, who clearly didn't get the reference.

'You and Alexei are a couple of drama queens,' JJ told his sister, then grinned. 'Actually, it's me who's having an existential crisis.'

'You? Why?' asked Alisha.

'Well, you guys are having them and I feel left out,' he said.

Alisha rolled her eyes and turned to me. 'India is the land of spirituality. Lots of wise people live there. Maybe I could even get enlightened.'

Now it was JJ's turn to roll his eyes. 'In under a week? I don't think so, sis. You can't go into a shop, pay your money and glug it down, like, I'll have a cherry soda and ... oh, I'll take a litre of enlightenment too.'

'Says who? What do *you* know?' said Alisha.

'There are books on it,' JJ replied. 'I've read about it. Like the big question of where true happiness lies, etc., etc. Philosophers, theologists and teachers have been musing about it for centuries.'

Alisha scoffed. 'Happiness to you is a bag of jelly beans. End of.'

'Jelly beans?' I asked.

Alisha nodded. 'JJ's favourite. Mom won't let us have too much sugar so JJ has to smuggle them in, then he sits and eats a whole packet at a time.'

JJ looked sheepish. 'My guilty secret. Thanks for telling everyone, Alisha.'

Like most siblings, JJ and Alisha love to wind each other up. I could see that they were gearing up for one of their arguments so I decided to butt in. 'So India, hey?' I said. 'How long for?'

'Not long. About six days. The director wants to add another scene into the movie so Dad has to stay longer than he expected. It'll be an evening shoot, then there's a wrap party for the end of filming the next night,' said JJ.

'How fabulous,' I said. It didn't feel fabulous at all; it felt rotten. Now I really did feel an existential crisis coming on.

'So, it's my birthday next week,' JJ continued, 'and I was going to do something here but now that Dad has to stay in India, he wants the family to join him and he said I can celebrate my birthday there.'

I nodded. 'I hope you have a great time,' I said. 'Maybe we can do something when you get back.' I decided to leave my list in my pocket. My options seemed so dull in comparison to where he was going.

JJ glanced at Alisha and grinned. He didn't seem a bit bothered about not spending his birthday with me. In fact, he seemed delighted about the idea. *Maybe we're not such an item after all*, I thought. *Maybe I'm much more into him than he is into me.*

JJ took my hand. 'When I get back,' he said, then grinned again. 'When *we* get back.' He squeezed my hand when he said 'we'. 'I've spoken to Mom and Dad and asked if, seeing as it's my birthday, I can invite you.'

It didn't sink in for a moment, I was so preoccupied with my disappointment.

'Did you hear what I just said?' JJ persisted.

'Yes, you're going to India.'

'He's asking if you'll come too,' Alisha said. 'Wake up and smell the curry! And no way am I going to be a gooseberry so I asked Mom and Dad if Pia could come as well and they said yes.'

This time, it did sink in. I glanced back up at the wall where a photograph of a lake at sunset still filled the screen.

'Me? Pia? India?'

JJ nodded. 'Yeah. What do you say? Just for five or six days? Mom'll take care of all the arrangements.'

I was stunned. I'd only ever been out of England a few times and that was to Europe when Mum was still alive. But India? Travelling with the Lewises? Time alone with JJ? It could be amazing. It *would* be amazing.

'It's a no-brainer. Of course I'd *love* to come.' I stared at the image on the screen and let myself imagine being there. To my left, I noticed Alexei hadn't said much and was looking thoughtful. 'You OK, Alexei?'

He nodded, and then shook his head. 'Just thinking I vish I could be there vith you.'

'Come too,' said JJ. 'I'm sure Mom and Dad won't mind.'

Alexei shook his head. 'I have to go to Paris vith

my parents. It is my aunt's birthday so all family vill be there.'

'Paris is lovely,' said Alisha. 'But yeah, shame you can't come with us. That would've been a blast.'

'It vould. Like, vot am I going to do on my own over in France after birthday?' asked Alexei.

'You'll be fine,' said Alisha, 'and we'll all be back here before you know it.'

'I guess,' Alexei replied, but he looked as disappointed as I'd felt only moments before.

'Can I see the slideshow again?' I asked.

'Of course,' said JJ.

'It'll be great to have you along,' said Alisha, as beautiful image after beautiful image appeared on the wall. 'We'll have such a top time.' She stuck her tongue out at her brother. 'We can get enlightened together. All my mates are getting into it back in LA. Used to be everyone had a psychiatrist but now the in-thing is to have a guru.'

'I thought they all had plastic surgeons,' said JJ and twisted his nose.

'Not me,' said Alisha. 'My nose is perfect and all my own.'

'Hey, I have to tell Pia,' I said. 'That is if she's awake!'

'Yeah, get her up here,' said Alisha. 'JJ insisted on telling you first but let's break the news to her, too.'

I quickly sent Pia a text telling her to come up urgently and she sent one back saying that she was on her way.

'Must have finally woken up,' I said as I clicked my phone off.

As we waited for her to arrive, JJ told me more about the trip and talked me through the pictures of temples, hotels and palaces. I felt dizzy with excitement. It looked so colourful and exotic and sounded so wonderful ... but then I remembered. Dad. GCSEs. Would he let me go?

A sinking feeling in my gut said, *Nnnnnnno*. N for no. N for never. N for *no way*.

3

Bollywood Babes

Pia and I sat in the kitchen at her house.

'How can life be so absolutely brilliant one moment and so totally rubbish the next? All in the space of twenty-four hours?' I asked. 'I feel like I've been on a rollercoaster inside my head.'

'Way less than twenty-four hours,' said Pia. She checked her watch. 'It's only one o'clock. So only two hours since I heard about India.' She slumped down and put her forehead on the table. 'Arghhhh.'

'It's like telling us we've won the lottery then saying, actually, it was a mistake. We haven't.'

After Pia had heard about her invite, we'd raced

down from the Lewises, Pia to tell her mum, and me to tell my dad.

'India? *Easter? This* Easter? No way,' Dad said, exactly as my gut had predicted.

'You do make me laugh,' Pia's mum told her.

We'd tried our full repertoire of persuasion.

Begging. (*Pleeeeeeeeeeeeeeeease.*) Pia told me she even went down on her knees. Her mum said that while she was down there, she might as well clean under the kitchen table. Parents think they're *so* funny sometimes.

Tears. (*Boo hoo, sob, warghhh.*) Dad looked like he wanted to run a mile.

Bribery. ('I'll wash the dishes for the rest of the year.') We were both told we should be doing that anyway in return for having a roof over our heads, getting fed, yadah yadah . . .

Clever arguing. (The school of life. It will be such a great experience . . .) 'And so will studying,' said both our parents. 'You have to think of your future.'

And finally, war. ('It's so unfair! I hate you and will never speak to you again!') 'Good,' said Dad. 'Peace at last.'

'You said that last week,' said Pia's mum. 'So no change there, then.'

Dad said I'd thank him later when I got good GCSE results. As *if*.

'I guess I have to tell JJ and Alisha sometime,' I said.

Pia lifted her head off the table and nodded. 'Better tell them now.' She got up, fetched the phone and handed it to me. I punched in their number. Mrs Lewis answered and told me that JJ and Alisha had gone out shopping in Sloane Street.

'Can I pass on a message?' she asked.

'No, er, yes, er ... I'm so sorry, Mrs Lewis, but my dad says I can't come to India with you, and Pia's mum won't let her go either.'

Mrs Lewis sounded surprised. 'You can't come? Is there a problem?'

'No problem, that is ... well, it's just that we have our GCSEs coming up and our parents say we have to study.'

'Study? Is that right?' She paused as if thinking for a second. 'Yes, of course, exams are important.'

'I've tried everything,' I said. I felt awful. It was so generous of Mr and Mrs Lewis to have asked us. I hated having to say no.

'Hey, hon, I've got to go, my other line's ringing,' said Mrs Lewis. 'I'll tell JJ you called.'

She hung up and my mobile rang straight afterwards. It was Gran. She was with my Aunt Maddie.

'Want to come over?' she asked.

'Can't. Can't go anywhere, Gran. Dad wants to lock me up forever,' I said and I filled her in on the whole morning.

'Is that right?' she said, then came out with exactly the same line as Mrs Lewis. 'Exams are important.'

She didn't seem bothered that my hopes had been dashed either.

'Hey, P,' I said. 'Seems no-one cares that we've just been given the best offer of our whole lives and we've had to turn it down. It's a total bummer. No way am I going to study today. I'm going to rebel.'

'Me too,' she said. 'Let's run away. Er ... but maybe not forever, just for today. See, even though I hate her, Mum's doing a roast for lunch tomorrow and I can't miss that.'

'OK, we'll be back later today, then.'

'We're going to have to sneak out,' said Pia. 'Mum's at the spa but she thinks I'm working at home.'

'And Dad thinks I'm at yours working with you.'

'But we do deserve at least one Saturday off, so

come on.' Pia stood up and pointed outside. 'To the gate.'

I went to join her. 'And beyond.'

We snuck out and were halfway to the tube station when the heavens opened and it began to pour with rain. Neither of us had an umbrella, so our hair was plastered to our faces in minutes and our jackets and jeans were soaked through.

I turned my face up to the sky. 'Hey, God, if you're up there. We could be in India where the sun shines. Can't you do anything?'

Pia trudged on past me. 'I am so miserable,' she droned. 'I am queen of miserableness, in fact.'

I plodded after her. 'Me too. What *is* our life? Trapped at home with two mean prison warders or out here in the rain getting soaked to the skin?'

Pia's mobile rang. She pulled it out of her pocket and glanced at the number. 'It's prison warder number one. Mum. What shall I do?'

'Ignore it,' I said, as my mobile rang. It was prison warder number two. Dad. I ignored him too.

As we walked along the road getting wetter by the second, I started to feel anxious. If Dad had realised I wasn't working at Pia's, he'd be well mad and I didn't want to suffer the Wrath of Mr Strictie-Pants for the whole holiday. Pia glanced at me. I could tell she was thinking the same thing.

'We're going to be *so* grounded,' she said. 'Perhaps we'd better take the calls, then go back, otherwise we might never be allowed out for the rest of the holidays.'

'My thoughts exactly. We need to handle your mum and my dad right if we're to get any time off for good behaviour.' When my phone rang again seconds later, I answered. 'Dad. Hi.'

'Where do you think you are?'

'I *think*, in fact I *know*, where I am. I'm on the pavement outside the chemist's.'

'Less of the cheek, Jess. And what are you doing there when you should be studying – and is Pia with you?'

I glanced in the window. I had to think fast. 'Fish oils! We're getting fish oils. Gran said they improve your brain-power.'

Pia gave me a thumbs-up then took the call from her mum. She gave her the same explanation.

After we'd squirmed our way out of not being at home with our books, we started to head back to Porchester Park.

'Let's do the misery shuffle,' said Pia and she drooped her shoulders, turned the corners of her mouth down and walked really slowly, dragging her feet. I followed along behind, my right hand on her shoulder, as if we were in a chain gang with manacles around our ankles. 'Woe, O woe,' I droned.

Pia joined in the droning with me. 'Woe, O woe,' she groaned.

'Let's do it in Russian,' I said.

'Voe, voe, oh voe,' we chorused in our best Russian accents.

A few passers-by stared at us which set me off laughing. Of course this only egged Pia on. She made herself look even sadder and she dragged herself forward like she had the cares of the whole world on her shoulders.

'Cheer up, love,' called a bald man from his van. 'It can't be that bad.'

'It is,' called Pia after him as he drove on. 'You have *no* idea.'

By this time, I was creased up laughing. 'Life's too short to be miserable,' I said. 'Come on, my strange little friend. I have an idea. Let's get home and get dry, then I'll tell you what it is.'

*

As soon as we got back to my house, I got out a take-away menu and ordered chicken curry, rice and lentils. Dad always lets us have a takeaway of some sort at the weekend so he couldn't object. I ran upstairs to get two towels to dry our hair and, while I was up there, I grabbed the sandalwood joss sticks that I bought at Camden Lock a few weeks before. A quick stop in Charlie's room to find a CD and I was almost ready. Back into my room to rummage under the bed and I had what I was looking for – two long pieces of shiny red curtain fabric. I took my load downstairs and put the CD on. Charlie had music from every country in the world and this was his Bollywood compilation. As the vibrant music began to pulsate through the room, I threw Pia a piece of fabric and a towel. She got the idea straightaway and we both wound the fabric around us sari-style, then wrapped our hair in the towels to make turbans. She whipped out a lipstick from her bag and put a red spot on my forehead and one on her own. I lit the joss stick and soon the sweet, woody scent filled the room. 'If we can't go to India, then India can come to us! Curry's on its way and maybe we can find a Bollywood movie on one of the channels on telly later.'

Pia wasn't listening. The music had got to her and she was too busy rotating her hips, stomping her feet and waving her arms in the air as she sang along to the CD at the top of her voice. '*Om shanti om.*'

'*Om shanti om,*' I joined in. We soon had a routine worked out. It was pretty good too. Thrust chest forward, wiggle, side-step, side-step, jump, stomp, push hands forward in the palm position and yell, '*OM SHANTI OM.*' Turn, wiggle, arms up right, arms up left, stomp to the music. '*OM SHANTI OM.*'

'What does *om shanti* mean?' I shouted over the music.

'Sort of "yo, peace, babe",' Pia called back.

We didn't hear the door open, nor Dad come in. 'TURN DOWN THIS RACKET!' he bawled and went over to the player and turned the music off.

He was with Gran and Aunt Maddie who both had puzzled expressions on their faces.

'What on *earth* do you think you're doing?' asked Dad, as Gran and Aunt Maddie took off their raincoats and hung them by the door. 'You could probably hear that music as far down the road as Harrods.'

I tried to straighten my face and look serious but a quick glance at Pia and I could see that she was having a hard time not cracking up. Her shoulders were beginning to shake with suppressed laughter as they always did when she knew she had to keep it together.

'Um, homework,' I spluttered, as Pia had a coughing fit next to me.

'And what kind of homework involves dressing up in the curtains and screaming your head off?' Dad persisted.

'They were just letting off steam, weren't you, girls?' Gran intervened, ever the peacemaker. Just like my mum used to, she liked a bit of Bollywood and I bet she would have joined in if Dad hadn't turned the music off.

'And I thought their movements were good,' said Aunt Maddie, just as there was a knock at the door. She did a few impressive hip wiggles herself which wasn't surprising because she did Egyptian dancing at night classes.

Dad wasn't amused. He went to the door to find Mrs Lewis standing there. 'Ah. Yes. Come in,' he said.

Mrs Lewis stepped inside. She always looked so effortlessly glamorous with perfect glossy hair and, today, a black trouser suit. She seemed rather out of place in our messy house. But she took one look at us and burst out laughing. 'Ah, getting ready for the trip, I see.'

'Er ... no, just ...' How could I explain? I always danced about like a demented whirling dervish and dressed up in the curtains on Saturdays? Probably not. And anyway, what was she on about? The trip was off.

Dad looked at Pia and me. 'Sit down, both of you,' he said.

Oh, here it comes, I thought. *Grounded. Another lecture on the joys of studying.*

Pia and I sat down at the breakfast bar and took the towels off our heads. I almost burst out laughing again because Pia's hair was standing straight up in wet clumps as if she'd gelled it.

Aunt Maddie, Gran and Mrs Lewis stood in a line next to Dad.

Dad sat on a stool at the bar with Pia and me and sighed. 'There's been a change of plan,' he said, and looked at the three very different women standing in front of him. Gran with her white bob, dressed in a turquoise tunic and jeans; Aunt Maddie with her chestnut hair, green cardigan and velvet skirt and Mrs Lewis, all chic and smart. 'It seems I've been ganged up on.'

'What do you mean?' I asked.

'Mrs Lewis came to see me after you'd gone out today. She's promised to personally oversee your studies each morning and make sure that you're never out without their minder.'

Mrs Lewis nodded. 'Our security is the best there is and I know it would mean a lot to Alisha and JJ to have your company.'

I glanced hopefully at Pia. 'And your grandmother and aunt were on the phone in an instant after you'd spoken to them.' He held up his hands. 'I give up. One female I could possibly argue with, but three? And *these* three? All assuring me that they know that exams are important but so is this trip. I can't win. All of them insist that you go to India. It's apparently an opportunity of a lifetime that can't be missed. What can I say?'

I could hardly breathe. 'You could say yes. *Have* you said yes, Dad?'

Dad nodded. 'I have, Jess. You can go.'

I was aware of Pia sitting next to me. He'd said I could go! 'What about—' I began.

'And you can go too, Pia,' Dad continued. 'I've spoken with your mother and so has Mrs Lewis. She's agreed to let you go too but you must *both* give me your word, and I mean it, that you won't neglect your studies.'

'We promise,' we chorused as I flicked the music back on and got up to dance the Bollywood stomp again. This time Gran joined in. A knock at the door distracted me and, when I went to open it, there was a disgruntled-looking Grace with two brown paper bags. 'I believe someone ordered a takeaway,' she said, and wrinkled her nose in disgust as she handed the aromatic bags over to us. 'It was delivered to reception.' She looked over at Dad. 'Which is *not* the place for takeaways!'

'No. Sorry, Grace,' said Dad. 'It won't happen again, *will* it, Jess?'

'No. Sorry,' I said as I took the curry from her. 'It should have come to the side gate. Mmmm.' I turned back inside when she'd gone. 'Brilliant. So, who's for a samosa?' Not even having upset Grace could spoil my mood now.

Hah, I thought, as Pia grinned at me. *Thank you, Gran. Thank you, Aunt Maddie. Thank you, Mrs Lewis. Sometimes I love Dad's motto. What a resident wants, a resident gets. Yay! India, here we come!*

4
Flight of Fantasy

'The Lewis family are bound to fly first class but I expect we'll be at the back,' said Pia. 'Which is OK for me because I'm titchy but you might feel cramped after ten or eleven hours sitting with your knees tucked into your chest.'

'I don't mind,' I said, as I packed the last of my toiletries. 'I'm just so excited to be going.'

'Me too,' said Pia, 'but I hope we get some sleep otherwise we're going to be zonkerooed when we get there.'

The past week had been a whirlwind of activity. Getting Pia's passport renewed. Getting our visas fast-tracked. Planning our wardrobes – it was going to be hot, hot, hot over in India. And trying to fit in some study time amidst it all to keep Dad happy. Though it was hard to focus on schoolwork when all I could think about was the trip away.

'Us in Rajasthan . . . I still can't believe we're really going!' I said. Just saying the word 'Rajasthan' conjured up a rush of exotic images in my mind.

I felt bad saying goodbye to Charlie because I was getting this mega treat and he was left behind in the UK, but he was cool about it. More than cool, actually – I could tell he wasn't going to miss me one bit! On the evening that we were leaving to get the night flight, he was in such a hurry to get out the house to meet my friend Flo, he hardly even said goodbye. They were off to see a movie. He and Flo got together recently, though she's had a crush on him for years. Pia felt guilty leaving Henry too, but he insisted that he wouldn't have it any other way, as long as she didn't try to get off with any Indian princes or attempt to impress people with her Bollywood dancing. He did ask her to bring him back a suitcase full of presents, though.

Alexei came down to join the others in waving us off before heading off on his own trip to Paris. I could

46

tell that he still wished he was coming with us. He stood in the forecourt with Dad, Pia's mum and Henry, as we got ready to get into the waiting Mercedes limo.

Henry started messing about and pretending to cry, so Pia thumped him. 'Ow,' he said.

'It's how I show affection,' she said, and gave him a big hug. Henry is built like a rugby player and Pia looks tiny beside him, but despite the difference in height, they make a great-looking couple: Henry with his square jaw and open face and Pia with her pretty pixie features.

I gave Dad a hug, then turned to Alexei. 'Find me an Indian princess,' he whispered.

Pia, who never missed a thing, turned to him and squeezed his arm. 'What good would she be to you in India, you dozo?'

'Dozo? Vot is dozo?' he asked.

'You are. Not thinking straight,' said Pia. She pointed at her head. 'What good would she be in India?'

'My parents have private plane. No problem,' he replied, then grinned. 'So not so dozo.'

I laughed. It really is another world for the Porchester Park residents.

Any feelings of remorse at leaving Dad and the boys disappeared as soon as we got into the car. As Mr Lewis was already in India, it was just Alisha, JJ, Mrs Lewis, Pia and me sitting back in the sumptuous leather seats as the limo purred its way through the dark streets to the airport. Another car had whisked away Vanya and our luggage and I couldn't help but be pleased to see the back of the canvas suitcase I had borrowed from Aunt Maddie. It looked so tatty in comparison to the expensive matching cases of the Lewis family. But I didn't dwell on it.

Pia and I had made a pact that we weren't going to stress about what they had and what we didn't. It was just a fact. They were loaded and we weren't, and we weren't going to let that spoil our holiday. As soon as we'd started packing for the trip, we'd realised that our swimming stuff was pretty shabby, we'd outgrown most of our summer clothes from last year and anything new that we'd bought had come from a sale or a second-hand shop. After an afternoon of meltdown we realised that we had a choice. Go on holiday with the Lewises and feel like the poor relations the whole time or go along and have a blast. Having a blast won.

'They're not inviting us for our money or our

clothes, babe,' said Pia when she saw me counting up my pocket money and the bit of cash Gran, Dad and Aunt Maddie had given me for the trip. 'They invited us because we're good, fun people. They like us and we like them.'

I'd been worried that we'd have to contribute to meals or trips out and would never be able to keep up, but Pia said that none of that mattered. Her attitude was that having good pals is what makes us the richest people on the planet, not how much cash we have. I was so glad she was coming with me.

I'd flown before but only short hops to Europe when Mum was still alive. I love travelling and airports, cruising the shops in anticipation of the flight, picking out a book or magazine to read on the journey, and I was looking forward to that stage of the trip. Also, I still hadn't found a birthday present for JJ so I was hoping to get him something in duty free.

It was a quiet car ride. Pia texted Henry, Alisha texted her mates in LA, Mrs Lewis was busy on her iPad and JJ had a Kindle so was reading one of the many books he'd downloaded to pass the time, books about Udaipur and the history of India. He looked over at me every now and again and smiled. At one point, he got out his phone and sent me a text saying one word.

Later.

I smiled back at him. I knew what he meant. We'd have time alone when we got to India. It gave me a happy glow inside that he'd texted the message. It felt like we had a secret and that, although we were with other people, there was something private happening between the two of us. I was also glad to see that the Lewises had dressed down for the flight in casual clothes and trainers – albeit pale pink Calvin Klein casuals in Alisha's case, and black and grey Armani in JJ's. Pia and I had wondered if we ought to wear our best clothes to travel in but, in the end, we'd worn jeans and T-shirts, figuring that if we wore our best, it would only get creased. So far, so good and no fashion faux pas.

'What time does our flight leave?' I asked Mrs Lewis.

'When we get to the airport,' she replied.

'I see,' I replied, none the wiser.

As we reached the motorway and began passing signs for Heathrow I felt another rush of excitement. I could tell that Pia was feeling the same. She squeezed my hand and whispered, 'And so our adventure begins!'

I was about to reply when we zoomed straight past the airport turnoff. Pia and I looked at each other then at Alisha, who was chatting away to her mum. JJ was lost in his own thoughts, gazing out of the window.

The driver must know where we're going, I thought as the car continued on. In the distance to our left, I could see lights blazing in the maze of airport buildings but we sped on past. I was just wondering whether to yell, 'Turn around!' when the car slowed down and the driver pulled up in front of what looked like a small but smart hotel. Pia looked at me and shrugged. She was as mystified as I was.

A blonde lady in a smart turquoise uniform came out and greeted Mrs Lewis through the rolled-down limo window, then she slipped into the seat beside the driver. I noticed a sign that said *VIP Terminus* and nudged Pia to look at it as we set off again. A few minutes later, we stopped alongside a small, sleek, white plane.

Alisha grinned. 'OK, girls. This is us.'

It took a moment to sink in as we all got out of the limo.

'It's a private jet!' I gasped.

JJ gave me a thumbs-up. 'Come on,' he said, and began to walk towards the plane where Vanya, blond and smart in a black suit, was waiting at the bottom of the steps.

'But . . . don't we have to check in?' asked Pia.

'No,' said Alisha.

JJ came back and linked arms with me. 'We just get on and we go.'

'On that?' I asked.

JJ turned to his sister. 'Didn't you tell them?'

'And spoil the surprise?' Alisha replied, then turned to us. 'Like it?'

'*Love* it,' I said.

I glanced at Pia. We'd both thought we'd be hanging about the airport for hours before take-off. Clearly not. We were travelling with A-listers and I was cottoning on fast. You turn up and drive straight to your private jet. No fuss, no hanging about. You get on. You go.

Pia and I followed the Lewises up the steps into the jet. A smiling steward with brown wavy hair and dressed in a navy uniform welcomed us aboard and showed us inside.

'I'm Jonathan,' he said, 'and this is Maria.' The

lady who'd been with us in the car came up the steps behind us, followed by Vanya. 'We'll be looking after you on the flight. Just let either of us know if there's anything you need.'

'Thanks,' said Pia as she took a peek inside to the right. 'How about a reality check? I must be dreaming.'

Jonathan smiled. 'I hope you enjoy the flight.'

'Wow,' I gasped when I followed the others inside. I slumped into an enormous leather armchair and looked around. 'There's so much space!' We were in an elegant living room decorated in subtle stone colours. At the centre of the room was a coffee table stacked with glossy magazines.

'Gazow,' echoed Pia.

Alisha sprawled on one of the plush sofas and raised an eyebrow. 'Cool, huh?'

'JJ, why don't you show the girls around?' said Mrs Lewis. 'I'm just going to call your dad and tell him that we're on our way. I'll see you all shortly for take-off.' And she disappeared into the back of the plane. Vanya sat in a corner of the living room and picked up a magazine.

I felt like I'd entered a Porchester Park apartment with wings.

Alisha stayed where she was as JJ began his tour. 'Welcome aboard this Boeing 737,' he said as he paused to sneak a look at the brochure about the jet that he'd picked up from a coffee table. 'It has a sumptuously appointed eighty square metres of cabin space divided into compartments. As you see, we're here in the living room, decorated in soft tan with cream leather sofas and matching armchairs, and softly lit by dozens of tiny ceiling lights ... Now, if you'd like to follow me.'

'You sound like an eejit, bro,' said Alisha from the sofa.

JJ ignored her and beckoned Pia and me into the next room where there was a further group of plush armchairs. 'Watch this,' said JJ. He waved his arm and a panel slid silently back to reveal a huge TV screen. 'Our own private cinema. Nice, huh?'

'I suppose it will have to do,' said Pia and yawned.

JJ laughed. 'And continuing our tour ...' He led us into a modern dining room with white tulips on the table and a bowl of fresh fruit. 'Seats eight comfortably,' he said as we moved on. 'Next we have the business centre.' He knocked and opened the door. Mrs Lewis was at a desk Skyping her husband.

JJ waved at the screen. 'Hi, Dad. Everything OK?'

'Sure,' said the handsome face on the screen. 'How are the girls?'

'Great, they're with me,' said JJ. 'Want to say hi, Jess?'

I stepped forward. 'Hi, Mr Lewis,' I said and gave a self-conscious wave. I can't help it but whenever I see Mr Lewis I'm totally starstruck, which I suppose isn't really surprising seeing as he is one of the biggest stars on the planet.

'Hi,' said Pia. 'Can't wait to get to India.'

He beamed back his million dollar smile. 'I'll see you all soon. Say hi to Alisha for me. Y'all have a good flight, now.'

We left the office and headed towards the rear of the plane. 'Two bathrooms, left and right,' said JJ, and Pia and I had a quick peek inside to see spacious showers, a loo and a basin. Like the rest of the plane, they looked top quality and smelt clean and perfumed, not the usual boiled lemon and antiseptic aeroplane loo smell. 'And finally . . .' He opened the door into a kingsize bedroom with an ensuite marble bathroom. 'Mom and Alisha will be in here but we'll be sorted too, I assure you. The seats in the cinema go back so I can sleep in there with Vanya and the sofas in the lounge pull out into beds for you girls.'

'What about Jonathan and Maria?' asked Pia.

'They have places up at the front of the plane, near the kitchen,' JJ replied.

'It's amazing,' I said as we went back through to the sitting room to join Alisha.

'It's really comfortable,' said JJ, 'especially for a long flight. Plus the plane has wifi so you can email or Skype your dad if you want to let him know how you're doing.'

'One jet we went on even had a disco onboard,' said Alisha, who seemed to be enjoying our awe. 'Can you imagine, dancing away as you fly through the clouds?'

'Insane,' I said.

Jonathan came through. 'If you wouldn't mind taking your seats, we'll be taking off in a few minutes and then you can roam, watch a movie or sleep,' he said.

'What would you like to do?' JJ asked us.

'I doubt I'll be able to sleep just yet. So, cinema room?' I said. It was cosy in there. 'Maybe a movie? Unless you want to sleep?'

'A movie sounds perfect,' JJ agreed.

'Movie and snacks then a sleepover,' said Alisha. 'Yay!'

I laughed. This was going to be the most luxurious, unique sleepover ever.

Mrs Lewis came through and we took our places in the living area. Alisha sat with her mum on the sofa, while JJ, Pia, Vanya and I were in the chairs. We belted up and, soon after, we took off into the sky. As the jet engines thrust upwards, JJ reached across and took my hand. 'Do you mind flying?'

'Are you kidding? I love it,' I said, and gazed out of the window at the night sky and the sea of grey clouds below us.

'Some people get scared,' he said.

'Not me.'

Even so, he didn't let go of my hand.

As soon as we were cruising well above the clouds, we unbuckled our belts and Vanya took his place in a corner away from the rest of us and pulled out a book. He didn't say much but he seemed perfectly at ease with everyone. Jonathan came through with a tray laden with juices and plates of delicious-looking tiny canapés. He placed them on the table in front of us. 'Let me know if you require anything,' he said and handed each of us a menu. 'Perhaps some dinner?'

The Lewises shook their heads. 'We ate before we

left home,' said Mrs Lewis. 'Thank you, Jonathan. Pia? Jess? How about you?'

I'd love to have tried something from the menu but Gran and Aunt Maddie had been over earlier in the evening and we'd had a big goodbye supper of chicken and mashed potatoes. I was still stuffed from it. Pia and I both shook our heads. 'No, thanks,' I said.

'Thanks for the snacks though, Jonathan,' said Alisha.

She and JJ were always so polite to their staff, polite to everyone, in fact.

Pia looked over at me and winked as she helped herself to a canapé. I knew she was loving the whole experience as much as me.

After the snacks, we went into the cinema room where Mrs Lewis watched half of a movie with us, then went to bed. The rest of us weren't tired, even though it was one-thirty in the morning. Pia and I were buzzing with the novelty of it all and to sleep would have meant to miss some of what was going on. Alisha gave in around two a.m., leaving me, JJ and Pia listening to music. Vanya was already asleep in one of the chairs that turned into beds in the cinema room. JJ and I held hands some of the time and, though I'd have liked to have curled up on the chair with him, I didn't want to make Pia feel like she was being left out. There would be plenty of time to be alone with JJ later.

At around two-thirty, despite my resistance, my eyelids grew heavy and Pia was almost asleep, so JJ asked Maria to make up the beds for us. We finally snuggled down but even though the beds were comfortable with silk sheets and feather-light pillows, I slept fitfully. So, at eight o'clock UK time, I got up and tiptoed through to the rear of the plane to take a shower. I could never resist trying out divine-smelling gels and lotions. It's one of my favourite things. The others were soon up too and as Jonathan served us a breakfast of fresh fruit, cheese, jam and warm croissants, I almost forgot that we were flying. It felt more like hanging out at someone's house or being in a fab hotel; the only reminder that we were thousands of metres up in the air being when I looked out of the window and saw the earth so far below.

After breakfast, JJ beckoned me into the office. 'Come with me. I'm just going to check my emails – you can do yours too, if you like.'

Pia and Alisha seemed fine – they were messing

about with each other's make-up bags, trying out the contents. Most of Alisha's make-up was Chanel, while Pia's was a mix of makes: No 7, Mac, Bobbi Brown.

I followed JJ into the computer suite and sat by his side as he went through his email inbox. He didn't seem to mind that I was looking over his shoulder. He read a few messages and then his phone bleeped that he had a couple of texts.

'Alexei says hi. He's on his way to France,' said JJ. 'Says he wishes he was with us.'

'I don't think he knows *what* he wants half the time,' I said. 'Like, he went out with Flo for a while then said he didn't want a committed relationship, but now all he ever goes on about is wanting a girl-friend.'

'Maybe he just wants to meet the right one,' said JJ and looked deeply into my eyes in a way that made my insides liquefy. 'Nothing wrong with that.' He reached out for my hand just as Mrs Lewis came in to collect some papers, so putting an end to anything happening.

He glanced back at his phone and smiled at the screen as Mrs Lewis went back out. He showed me what he was looking at. It was an image of a stunning and curvy Indian girl who looked just a bit older than me.

'Who's that?' I asked.

'Shreya. Haven't you heard of her?'

I shook my head.

'She's a big star in India. A teen music sensation. Had her first hit when she was thirteen and now she's getting into acting. She's had a few scenes in the movie Dad's in.'

'Do you know her?'

'We've met a few times. Once in LA, once in India ages ago. She was just texting to say hi.'

I glanced back at the screen. It was more than hi. She'd written: can't wait to see you again. And she was beautiful, with a perfect body, perfect hair and a perfect smile. She seemed to be looking straight into me.

JJ must have noticed my reaction because he squeezed my hand. 'Hey, don't look so worried. She's just a friend, hardly even that.'

I squeezed back. 'I'm not worried.'

When JJ went to take a shower, I told Pia about the text.

'Who are you talking about?' asked Alisha when she came back in from her shower in the other bathroom.

'Someone called Shreya,' said Pia. 'She just texted JJ.'

'Oh her. She's always texting him. I wouldn't worry, Jess. She's way too high maintenance for him. Such a drama queen. Apparently she's been a real pain on the shoot. Always wanting to do it her way and no good at taking direction.'

'Why's she texting JJ?'

'She collects boys. Probably wants to add him to her list of conquests, but he's so not interested.'

We spent our last few hours on the plane reading glossy magazines and listening to music but as we took our seats for landing, my mind kept going back to the photo of Shreya. It niggled away at me. She collected boys. If there was nothing to worry about, then why was she sending JJ pictures of herself? It sounded to me like he was next on her hit list.

5

Udaipur

I started to fall in love with India the moment we left the airport. On the journey into town, the Lewises donned their shades then sat back in the car, as though the scenery we were driving through was nothing out of the ordinary, but Pia and I had our noses pressed up against the windows, taking it all in. Everything I looked at was worthy of a photograph. Indian women in jewel-coloured saris riding bicycles, children waving as we passed by, a lorry in front of us painted bright yellow, red and green and adorned with garlands and tinsel, carved temples and, above it all, the blue, blue sky.

The closer we got to the town, the more crowded the streets became and only a few drivers seemed to be sticking to any kind of lane system, or any kind of pavement. There were cars, taxis and buses all packed to bursting, with people hanging out of windows, others sitting on top of the vehicles, and all the time the traffic going in every direction and battling for space. There were more mopeds than I'd ever seen in my life, honking and tooting as they wove their way in and out of it all. *They certainly know how to share*, I thought, as I watched a family of four sail past on a moped, beeping their horn loudly as an ox almost walked into them. I wished I hadn't put my camera in my luggage because I wanted to record it all to show Charlie and Dad when I got back. I quickly snapped a few photos with my phone, but they weren't up to much.

When we finally reached Udaipur, it seemed like the whole world was out on the streets; not just cars, bikes, buses and mopeds, but also open taxis that JJ told us were called auto rickshaws or tuk tuks, which swerved their way in-between the rest of the traffic, narrowly missing each other.

'Oh my God!' I gasped, as I noticed an elephant stroll by, followed by a family of pigs who scuttled under him then dived down an alleyway like they knew exactly where they were going. And soon there were cows, dogs and chickens too.

'You could never feel lonely here,' Pia commented, as we passed a group of men sitting at a table, smoking and chatting, their stalls behind them overflowing with clothes, scarves, bags and art prints. 'Everyone lives and works outside, unlike the UK.'

'Probably because of the sun,' I said, as I looked up and saw an enormous film poster featuring Shreya beam down at us from ten metres up in the air.

Pia nudged me. 'Big sister is watching yooooou,' she whispered.

A sharp left took us down a quieter street, then we reached the arrival area for our hotel. As we drove into the car park on the shores of Lake Pichola, it felt like an oasis of calm after what we had just come through.

'It's like going from a fridge into a sauna,' I said as we got out of the cool, air-conditioned car into the baking sunshine. I glanced at my watch. It was just after five in the afternoon, Indian time. Pia took a photo with her camera-phone of the vehicle that had brought us from the airport. It was a maroon and cream vintage Bentley with soft leather seats inside.

Fabulous. Pia sent the photo off to Henry. He'd love it and so would his dad. Cars were their thing.

A tall Indian man in white turban and gold Indian-style uniform stood with a large fringed parasol outside a small tent-like building next to the lake, which sparkled in the late afternoon sun. He came forward to greet us and ushered Mrs Lewis inside. 'Won't be moment,' she said over her shoulder.

JJ took my hand and led me over to the lake. He pointed at a white marble and mosaic palace glistening in the centre of the water.

'That's the Taj Lake Palace,' he said. 'Remember it from the slideshow?' he asked.

It looked like a giant two-tier wedding cake with pillars and arches around the sides. 'That's the hotel we'll be staying in,' he said. 'It was originally built around 1743 as the royal summer palace and covers the whole island, which is why is appears to be floating.'

The hotel and view were straight out of a fairytale. I glanced at JJ. Tall and handsome with a high forehead and sculpted cheekbones, he was dressed in a white T-shirt and linen trousers and was wearing his usual Ray-Ban shades. *He has a noble face*, I decided. *I have to be dreaming. Me, Jess Hall, staying in a real palace. And I have my very own prince to hang out with.*

'Cool, huh?' said Pia, coming to join us.

'It's beautiful,' I agreed.

Alisha nudged her brother. 'JJ's Mr Norman Know-It-All,' she teased. 'He knows all about the history of this place – in fact, anywhere we go in the world.'

JJ smiled. 'So? I like history. And did you know this hotel was used as a location for the movie *Octopussy*?'

'The Bond film?' asked Pia. 'I've seen that!'

JJ nodded. 'It was also used in a TV series called *The Jewel and the Crown*.'

I looked out over the view again. 'It's stunning,' I said. 'Heavenly.' On one side of the lake were mountains, on the other, to our right, was an even bigger palace than the one in the middle of the water. It was vast, the white walls turning a honey-rose colour in the late afternoon sun, and it appeared to go on forever with domed turrets, terraces and balconies overlooking the lake. 'What about that place?'

JJ followed my gaze. 'That's the City Palace,' he replied. 'Actually, it's a series of palaces, the first one built in 1559. There's a scene in Dad's movie which is being shot inside it, so I'm sure we'll have a chance to go and take a look around tomorrow before the cameras start rolling. It's amazing, full of great art and wall paintings. There are actually two hotels in there too. They used to be royal guesthouses. One of the palaces was apparently built in memory of a beautiful princess who poisoned herself to stop rival princes battling for her hand in marriage.'

'She *poisoned* herself?' asked Alisha.

'So the story goes,' said JJ.

Alisha rolled her eyes. 'I would have told them all to stop squabbling and get a life. Fancy killing yourself over a load of dumb boys.'

'Exactly,' said Pia. '*So* sixteenth century.'

'Lots of the hotels here used to be palaces, and homes to maharajas,' JJ said, 'and Udaipur is known as the most romantic city in India.' He squeezed my hand as he said 'romantic', a slight movement that Alisha clocked immediately.

She put two fingers in her mouth and fake-gagged. 'Oh God, slush alert. Are you two going to be mooning over each other the whole time we're here?'

I laughed but from the small bit of Udaipur I'd seen, I could already see why it was known for being romantic. It was the most beautiful place I'd ever been to and the City Palace had immediately captured my imagination. I wondered what had gone on there over the centuries – apart from the princess who'd poisoned herself – what other dramas and love affairs. *I am going to love it here*, I thought, as I got out my sunglasses. Even the weather felt perfect: sunshine with a gentle breeze. I breathed in deeply, I wanted to remember this moment forever. All I needed to make it a hundred per cent perfect would be some time alone with JJ, maybe on a balcony at one of the palaces, maybe on a terrace overlooking the lake.

'The boat's ready,' Mrs Lewis called from inside the tented area, so we trooped in to join her and Vanya who had travelled in a car just behind ours.

Minutes later, we took our places in a small speedboat which was open at the sides but canopied on top. The padded seats were covered with Indian cushions and we sat back to enjoy the ride.

'What a great way to get there,' I said, as we whooshed through the water towards the hotel.

'It's the *only* way to get there,' said JJ. 'The hotel owns the boats. They don't allow non-residents to come ashore, unless they are guests of people staying there, so you can't just pop over for a look around.'

'I really do feel like I'm in a Bond movie,' said Pia,

as she stood up and let the breeze blow through her hair.

Alisha stood beside her. '*You only live twice . . .*' she sang. 'Dad was in one of the Bond movies, you know. Just a small part, before he was really famous.'

'Will he be at the hotel?'

'He will,' said Mrs Lewis. 'Maybe we can get some tea, then I suggest we all order room service and get an early night as I doubt any of us slept much last night.' She looked at Pia, then me. 'And you two have to keep your minds fresh for studying.'

Pia grimaced. 'I'd forgotten about that.'

Mrs Lewis raised an eyebrow and smiled. 'Well, I hadn't. I promised your parents.'

JJ shot me a glance. 'I . . . I might show Jess around a bit if that's OK,' he said.

Behind him, and out of their mother's line of sight, Alisha turned away from us and wrapped her arms around herself, doing a mock smooch. Pia cracked up and JJ smiled. I knew he was thinking the same as I was. Time alone in the most romantic city in India . . . Who wouldn't want it? It seemed like we'd have to wait, though, because Mrs Lewis shook her head. 'Plenty of time for looking around tomorrow,' she said. 'I'm not only headmistress for your stay but also your chaperone.' She was smiling as she said it but I knew she was serious too. Dad wouldn't have let me travel to the other side of the world unless he felt completely confident that I wouldn't be left alone, especially with a teenage boy, even if he *was* JJ Lewis.

Our boat arrived at the hotel jetty where an Indian man in a red turban and smart navy traditional uniform stepped forward to help us up onto the wide marble terrace outside the hotel. A red carpet led across the open area to the hotel reception, which we could see behind a wall of glass. From an open balcony on the floor above came a shower of rose petals, filling the air with their gentle scent. I looked up to see the smiling face of a young Indian girl. She put down her basket when she saw me look up. 'Welcome,' she called.

We stepped through an open door into the reception area where three ladies in green saris were waiting with round brass trays in their hands. One came forward and placed a garland of golden flowers around each of our necks. The second, who was carrying a lit candle on her tray, dotted red powder on our foreheads. The third handed each of us an iced pink drink in a tall glass. 'Passionfruit,' she said. 'You like.'

'Now *that's* what I call a royal welcome,' I whispered to Pia.

'I still feel like I'm in a movie,' she replied and peeled off her jacket. 'And it's so wonderfully hot here. Love, love, love it.'

The architecture of the hotel was a mix of old and new with white arches and pillars along corridors, Indian statues placed in alcoves, polished marble floors, open rooms leading into each other and ... Oh. My. God. It was Shreya, and she was coming our way. She looked like she'd stepped out of *Hello* magazine, dressed in wide white linen trousers and a low-cut, short, silk turquoise top showing off a perfectly toned midriff, with loads of silver bling on her ears and around her neck and a big smile on her perfect, goddess face.

'Hey, JJ,' she called and tottered towards us on impossibly high silver mules. She flung her arms around him, then turned to Alisha and air-kissed her. 'Alisha. *Mwah, mwah.*' I noticed that Alisha didn't *mwah, mwah* Shreya back.

She exuded glamour from every pore. I stood there feeling like a lily-white frump in my crumpled shirt, jeans and scuffed red Converse.

'This is Jess and Pia,' said JJ.

Shreya looked us up and down. The tiniest flicker of an eyelid showed that she wasn't impressed but then she flashed us a big smile. 'Friends of Alisha's from England?'

JJ came and put his arm around me. 'Friends of both of ours.'

Again a flicker, this time of annoyance. She linked arms with JJ and pulled him aside. 'How fabulous,' she said over her shoulder to me and Pia. 'We're going to have such fun showing them around, aren't we, JJ?'

So much for getting time alone, I thought, as I pasted a smile on my face. 'Can't wait,' I lied.

6

The Rules

After we'd checked in, we had tea with the Lewises and Shreya in an area called the reading room. *All* the Lewises. Jefferson Lewis too. All six-foot-four, super-duper, charismatic, handsome movie star of him. The man definitely has the X factor. It's as if he's been polished to give off an extra glow the rest of us mortals don't have. Actually, that's not true; JJ has it too. He looks like a somebody. I always notice a few people looking at him when we're out in public.

I enjoyed the tea but it felt unreal being in such an amazingly pretty room with marble floors and arches along the wall inlaid with coloured glass patterns of flowers and plants. We sipped tea out of china cups, ate freshly-baked almond cookies and were waited on by smiling staff who were clearly as much in awe of Mr Lewis as I was.

Seated on the floor behind our table were three musicians, one beating tabla drums, one playing a sitar and one with a wooden stringed instrument that I didn't recognise. I wanted to ask what it was but I couldn't help feeling tongue-tied in front of Mr Lewis, even though he went out of his way to welcome me and Pia and put us at ease. I tried to relax but I couldn't get the fact out of my head that I was sitting with one of the biggest movie stars in the world, plus Shreya was talking enough for all of us. Pia was much better than I was and chatted away like she'd known Mr Lewis all her life, totally at home with him and her surroundings. Shreya did her best to monopolise JJ but he always tried to bring me into the conversation. She clearly didn't like that. I could tell that to her I was a nobody who was in her way, and I couldn't help feeling shy. When the waiter brought a tray with refills for the tea, I finally plucked up courage to ask about the musicians behind us. I pointed at the unfamiliar stringed instrument behind him.

'Excuse me. What's that?' I asked.

'A milkosi,' he said. At least, that what I *thought* he said.

'A milkosi. Oh, I've never heard of that before. How do you pronounce it again?'

'Milkosi,' the waiter repeated.

'I'll tell my brother,' I said. 'He's really interested in unusual musical instruments.'

The waiter looked baffled.

Shreya burst out laughing and pointed at the tray he had in his hand where there was a teapot and a little silver jug, both covered with a tea cosy. 'Mi*lk* cosy,' she said. 'A milk cosy. We use them here to keep the milk warm, as well as the tea.'

The waiter had thought I was pointing to the jug on his tea tray. I felt so stupid and went bright red. 'Oh.'

Even the Lewises laughed, but JJ reached over and squeezed my hand. 'Easy mistake,' he said.

Shreya wouldn't let it go. 'Milkosi. Mil*kosi*,' she kept repeating. 'Hysterical. I love it.'

Pia flashed me a look of sympathy. She knew I got nervous around people sometimes and acted like an idiot.

Alisha didn't seem to have much time for Shreya

at all and virtually ignored her to talk with her dad and Pia.

When Mrs Lewis repeated her earlier suggestion that we go to our rooms, unpack, order room service and get an early night so we'd be fresh for the morning, I was glad to get away from Shreya. Alisha and JJ seemed happy with the suggestion too and disappeared off to their own rooms with a promise to catch up in the morning.

Pia and I were bowled over when we saw our room and, although at tea I'd felt out of sorts, seeing where we were staying gave me a fresh burst of energy and all thoughts of the stupid milk cosy were forgotten. Mrs Lewis said she'd picked the room especially with us in mind and it was perfect, decorated in pink and gold, with ivory and gold bedspreads on divinely comfortable beds. It also had an alcove with a table and two chairs where we could sit and work and a padded window seat where we could look out over the lake to the City Palace.

'I don't know if I can take roughing it like this much longer,' said Pia through the open door of the bathroom in our room a short time later, where she was soaking up to her neck in a bath of jasmine-scented bubbles, with a glass of sparkling elderflower juice on the side and a lotus-shaped candle burning on a ledge by the basin.

'I know,' I replied. 'It's a tough life, isn't it?' I was lying on an enormous bed, wrapped in one of the hotel's white fluffy towelling robes, my skin all perfumed and soft after a bath where I'd used every body product I could find.

'So, what do you want to happen with JJ on this holiday?'

I got up to look out of the window. Across the water, the lights of Udaipur twinkled. 'For us to visit all the most romantic spots in the area. Have some time *alone*. Oh. I don't mean leave you out, but—'

'I know what you mean, dozo. I'd be the same if Henry was here. We're in the city of romance, you've got to make the most of it. Mates come first, we both know that, but I have Alisha, so don't worry about me. What else?'

'Get to know him better,' I replied. 'Have him fall totally in love with me and write poems about me so that I'll be immortalised forever.'

Pia laughed. 'You don't want a lot, then.'

'I'm joking about being immortalised. I don't know. Basically not to blow it. Don't forget I'm a relationship newbie.'

'You're worried about Shreya, aren't you?' said Pia, as she got out of the bath and wrapped herself in a huge bath towel that had been laid out in the bathroom. She padded in to join me, threw herself back on her bed which, like mine, had been covered in red rose petals like those showered on us in reception. She propped herself up with cushions.

'A bit,' I replied. 'I mean, she's stunning and she was clearly put out by the fact that he'd brought me along.'

'Trust,' said Pia. 'I think it's number one in any relationship. Can he trust you?'

'Definitely.'

'Do you trust him?'

'I think so.'

'So chill. Rule one in the book of keeping a relationship alive is trust. Trust each other and in that trust, you can be secure that you're the One. Rule number two – don't get all needy and insecure the moment another girl comes along. There will *always* be other girls who will fancy JJ. I don't think you need to worry, though. He clearly only has eyes for you and no way would he have invited you all this way if he wanted something to happen with Shreya. Also, remember JJ isn't Tom.'

Tom is the babe magnet in the Sixth Form at our school. I'd had a crush on him ever since he arrived at the beginning of the school year and although he'd appeared interested and flirted for England at first, I soon found out that he was a player and didn't do commitment. All my hopes for anything happening with him had been well squashed when I found out that he'd been seeing Keira, a girl I used to know in junior school who had come back to live in London and seemed to have it in for me. Not just seemed to, she *did* have it in for me. She did her best to ruin any chance that I had with Tom and also in a modelling competition that we had both entered earlier in the year. Sadly for her, it all backfired and she was asked to leave the competition. She lost Tom too when he realised what she was really like. Lately Tom has been pursuing me again, saying he wants to get serious, but I don't trust him any longer. I'm pretty sure he only wants me because I'm with someone else now and he doesn't like that. He's the kind of boy who likes a challenge but I know that the moment I give in, he'll drop me and move on to another conquest. I'm not into playing games and part of the reason I like JJ so much is that he isn't either. He plays it straight and I do too. Tom still sends me texts, like he's fishing to see if there's any hope for us. I haven't told JJ about the messages but I don't feel that I'm being dishonest because I don't answer them. It isn't as if anything's happening with Tom or is ever going to.

'You're right,' I said, 'but I don't think Shreya sees it that way. I saw the way her face lit up when she saw JJ and how she didn't like it when she saw me. But OK, I get it. Rule one, trust. Rule two, don't be needy. What's rule three?'

'Enjoy being with each other,' said Pia. She looked around the room and spied the mini bar. 'Now, what haven't we tried out in here? I bet there's some chocolate ...'

As Pia raided the tiny fridge, someone pushed an envelope under the door. I leapt up, hoping that it might be a note from JJ. I ripped open the envelope. It was from Mrs Lewis. Our itinerary for the week, partly typed, partly handwritten.

I shook my head and sighed. 'Study, study, study,' I said as I read the message. 'Sorry, Pia. No trips out for us, I'm afraid.'

She got up and grabbed the paper from me, then picked up a pillow and biffed me with it.

She read the schedule out loud. '*Tuesday: morning,*

study. Bleurgh. No, we can do it. I suppose we have to if we're going to get good grades. *Afternoon, explore part of the City Palace.* Yay. *Evening,* oh my God! *Watch filming at the City Palace.* Did you see this, Jess? We get to go and see Jefferson Lewis in action!'

'Shreya's playing the Maharaja's daughter, isn't she?' I asked.

Pia nodded. 'A part I feel she plays in real life too,' she said, then read on. *'Wednesday: morning, study.* Hmm. Can't wait. *Afternoon, visit to Udaipur.* Wow. It gets better. *Treatments in the spa ready for the party. Evening, movie wrap party at the Shiv Niwas hotel which is in the City Palace complex.'*

She read on. Thursday morning was more study, followed by a trip to Jaipur. Friday morning, studying again, then exploring the region in the afternoon. Then on Saturday we were all going to Deogarh, to celebrate JJ's birthday with dinner on the Imperial Barge. Sunday was the day we headed home.

'Awesome,' said Pia. 'This is easily the most amazing place I've ever been to.'

'And it's only just begun,' I said.

Pia switched on the TV, sat back on the bed and began flicking channels. She finally settled on one showing Indian dancers doing line dancing. They were dressed in cowboy outfits but it was still pure Bollywood. 'Perfect,' she said, as she made herself comfy.

I looked at my watch. It said midnight but I wasn't tired as it was only around seven p.m. UK time and I hadn't adjusted to Indian time yet. 'I'm going to go for a bit of an explore. Might even go and find JJ,' I said. 'Want to come?'

Pia stretched and yawned. 'Not tonight. I can't be bothered with putting my clothes back on and I think I might try and Skype Henry before I go to sleep. But Jess, I'd leave JJ. Another rule about having a relationship is to give each other space. I think you need to be cool after today, not that I think you have anything to worry about with Shreya, but you need to show that it didn't bother you at all. You went to bed and slept without a care in your mind. Because *you* are the One.'

I stepped out onto the small balcony leading off the alcove and marvelled again at where I was. I felt like I'd stepped onto another planet. As I gazed over the water towards the City Palace, I wondered again what had gone on there. Who the people were who'd lived there and what their stories were. It looked so ancient. It *was* so ancient. A few boats with soft lights moved around the lake under a canopy of stars. The whole atmosphere was completely magical.

A movement to my left made me realise that there was someone on the jetty, where a boat was waiting. As my eyes adjusted to the dark, I saw that it was JJ with, by the shape of the other person, Shreya. Before she got onto the boat, she moved towards him.

Move away, move away, I urged him in my mind. But he didn't and next thing I knew, I was watching my boyfriend embrace one of India's most stunning teen stars.

So, go to bed? Sleep? Not a care in my mind? I am the One? Somehow, I didn't think so.

7
Alone with JJ

The next day Pia and I went to the restaurant for breakfast, expecting to see the Lewises there. We soon realised that they had their meals in their rooms.

'Of course,' said Pia, as we surveyed the sumptuous spread of foods laid out on a central table: fresh fruit of every kind, juices, breads, cereals, yoghurt, cheese, ham, salami, croissants, pastries, plus the usual full English of eggs, sausage and bacon. 'They don't want the whole world ogling them and watching them eat, do they?'

'I guess not. Do *you* want to eat in our room?' I asked.

'Hell no,' said Pia, as she piled fresh mango into a white bowl. 'I want to use every bit of the hotel: the restaurants, the spa, the pool. I want to see everything, take it all in.'

'Me too,' I agreed, as I helped myself to a variety of berries then added yoghurt and honey. It felt a shame to eat in our room when there was so much to see. We took seats at a table looking over a lily pond in the courtyard in the centre of the hotel. In daylight, the water was a vivid turquoise against the white of the palace and I watched the numerous fountains gushing as we ate our fruit and were served fresh juices by smiling waiters. I thought about Charlie back home, eating his usual piece of toast at the breakfast bar in our little house. I wished he could have been here to share it all with me and vowed to buy him something wonderful to take back. Maybe a musical instrument . . . just not a milkosi.

My phone bleeped that I had a text.

Where R U? JJ.

I texted back: **Breakfast. Restaurant in courtyard.**

He replied. **C U in ur room in half an hour.**

'I think you were right,' I said as I showed Pia the text. 'I suppose they want to be private, even here in the hotel.'

Pia nodded. 'There are loads of suites in the hotel,' she said. 'I checked it out on the hotel website. Rich people must come here for privacy as well as location.'

I didn't tell Pia but I was worried about what JJ wanted to talk to me about. I hadn't told her why he hadn't come looking for me last night, that he'd been with Shreya instead. I pushed my bowl away. I'd suddenly lost my appetite. My stomach was full of butterflies and there was no room for food in there too.

JJ was waiting outside our room when we returned from breakfast. He was dressed in black jeans and a white linen T-shirt, immaculate as always. He beamed when he saw us and came and put his arm around me.

'How's it going so far?' he asked.

'Great,' I said as Pia opened the door to our room and let us all in. She turned around. 'Oh! I left my sunglasses in the restaurant,' she said, winked at me and disappeared. I knew she hadn't left her glasses at all. She was giving us space. At last, some time alone with JJ.

JJ flung himself down on Pia's bed. I was dying to

ask him about Shreya but remembered all Pia's advice about trust and not being needy so I bit my lip.

JJ sighed, like he wanted to say something difficult.

'Is something up?' I asked.

'Not really. I mean . . .' He beckoned me over to sit next to him. 'It's weird, isn't it?'

'What's weird?'

'Us. Being here. It's a bit unreal. Like, you're here with me but—'

'But what?' I blurted. I felt my stomach lurch in anticipation of being dumped for Shreya. I steeled myself for the news.

'But it's still early days with us and . . . I'm aware that you have Pia with you and Alisha here so of course you'll want to hang out with them. I don't want to be the possessive boyfriend and crowd you. I want to give you space but, hey, I want to be with you as well. Oh, I don't know. I don't know what I'm trying to say. I guess . . . I just don't want to blow it with you.'

My mouth dropped open. He'd said *exactly* what I'd been feeling. 'That's why *I* didn't call *you*. I wanted to give you space too.'

JJ laughed. 'Seriously? What a mad pair we are. If

we go on like this, we'll never get any time alone, not least because we have half a dozen chaperones most days!'

'We're alone now.'

JJ smiled and moved closer. I closed my eyes ready for him to kiss me when someone knocked at the door. We leapt apart and I got up to answer.

It was Mrs Lewis. She looked surprised to see JJ sitting on the bed. 'Jess, just checking in on you. JJ, what are you doing here?' She indicated with her thumb that he should leave. 'And where's Pia?'

Pia appeared behind her at the door. 'Here,' she said.

'I promised your parents you'd study,' said Mrs Lewis. 'So come on, get on with it. JJ, out you go. We're heading into town but we'll see you girls there later. Call if you need anything. Vanya will bring you across to join us later and you have all our cellphone numbers in case you need to call.'

Behind her, JJ raised an eyebrow and grinned, then Pia and I were left alone with our books. Studying was the last thing I felt like doing.

'Are relationships always like this?' I asked Pia.

'Like what?'

'Finding your way. Not being sure about the other

person's feelings, then discovering that they weren't at all what you thought?'

Pia nodded. 'That's the fun of it. The big lesson is *never* to assume that you know what's going on in your boyfriend's head. That's why all our girlie magazines always go on about communication in relationships. You have to keep talking to each other, otherwise it gets crazy. The number of times I've stressed myself out when I didn't hear from Henry and imagined he'd gone off me, then I talk to him and he looks at me like he has no idea what I'm on about, he's just been busy or something. Doing boy stuff. So yeah, keep talking.'

At last, our studying done, Vanya arrived to accompany us to meet the Lewises and, after another movie-star-style boat trip across the lake, we made our way towards town and through a triple-arched gate into the City Palace. Pia was wearing a red dress and sweet coral cardi and I was wearing a halterneck top, a blue skirt and sandals – nothing out of the ordinary, just clothes we'd chosen because they were light and it was so hot outside. But people still stared at us as we walked through the main gate to the City Palace. We spotted JJ waiting for us a short distance away. I so hoped that we'd get *some* time alone today, even if it was just a few minutes.

'JJ will accompany you around,' Vanya told us. 'He has a guide with him who can tell you about the history, and I won't be far away.'

'Thanks, Vanya,' said Pia.

'Where's Alisha?' I asked JJ when we reached him.

'Ah. She's hanging out at the pool at the Shiv Niwas hotel with Mum.'

'Didn't she want to see inside the palace?' asked Pia.

'Yes but . . . let's say the scenery at the hotel pool suddenly got more interesting,' he said as he led us towards the interior of the palace.

A text from Alisha as JJ was talking explained all.

Have met most divine boys. Their dad owns hotel on other side of lake. Am in lurve. C U l8r. A

'Do you mind me being here?' whispered Pia. 'I'd really like to see the palace but if you want to be alone with JJ, just say.'

I put my arm round her. 'I want to see it with *you*, my little munchkin.' Although I wanted time with JJ, no way was I going to forget the rule and put a boy before a mate.

For the next hour, we explored the many rooms

and floors of the City Palace with a young Indian guy called Ramesh as our guide. Vanya stayed with us but he always maintained a bit of distance to give us space.

'Awesome, awesome and awesome,' was all Pia managed to say as wonderful room opened into wonderful room on floor after floor. Every square centimetre was painted or carved or covered in mosaic – even the ceilings were painted in a riot of colour. Some walls had brightly coloured paintings of elephants or camels, others gods, goddesses or ancient rulers. The most impressive was an opulent, enclosed area in the centre of the palace called the Peacock Court. The floor was made up of black and white square tiles and the walls had tiered balconies up top so people could see down into the courtyard.

Ramesh pointed to a projected balcony. 'That is where the king used to address the court,' he told us as we looked up.

'Wow, I love this place,' I said, as I took in peacock mosaics on one side that had been made from green, blue and gold glass.

'Five thousand pieces of glass were used to make them,' said Ramesh. 'The peacock is the bringer of good luck. The works of art on the walls to your right depict scenes from the legends of the Hindu god, Lord Krishna.' I looked at the life-size depictions in all shades of gold glass. They were stunning.

'And look at those doors,' said Pia. One had rows of brightly coloured blue and green feathers painted around it; another gold door was set back in the wall with a series of deep green arches that seemed to ripple out towards us.

As we wandered through the maze of corridors, towers, courtyards, pavilions and rooms interlinked with pillars or arches, JJ took my hand and looked as impressed as me and Pia. 'I've never seen anything like this. Ornate is not the word. It even beats Porchester Park!' he said with a smirk, as he looked up at a gold and red mosaic ceiling. 'When was it built, Ramesh?'

'The palace was built 450 years ago by Maharaja Udal Singh, sir,' Ramesh told us, 'and has been added to by subsequent generations, which is why it is now a series of palaces, eleven in all, measuring two hundred and forty-four metres long and thirty metres high.'

Pia nodded, busy photographing everything she could. I think Ramesh had lost her with all his stats. I preferred to look rather than photograph. I could send Pia's pics back to Dad and Charlie.

'Seeing this place makes me feel like doing interior design,' I said as we walked through one room with arches to the right, pillars to the left all painted in soft blue with white, then on into another room decorated in soft green with gold mirrors and burgundy window frames and doors. Everywhere we went was a feast of colour: gold and orange rooms, pink, green and blue rooms, some gaudy and bright, others soft and subtle. Orange-red flowers were painted on a blue background. A gold elephant and camel on a turquoise wall. I glanced down to a courtyard where women in red, pink and cobalt blue saris were strolling, adding more splashes of colour to the already dazzling scene.

'Yeah, but you'd need clients who had a gazillion million to spend to recreate anything like this,' said Pia.

My favourite room had a wall of red and silver mirrors laid out in a zig-zag pattern, and a black and white tiled floor. It was insane but it worked.

'Do you think it's because of the sun here?' asked Pia. 'All the colours, I mean. In England so many people wear grey and black, especially in winter. Here everything is totally intense and brilliant.'

'Probably. It makes me want to throw out all my black clothes,' I said.

Just as we thought we'd seen it all, we entered a room where the walls were made from small squares of blue, orange, green and yellow glass. The afternoon sun streamed through creating the most amazing play of light.

'I've almost used up my whole photo card,' said Pia. 'We have to see if we can buy a book to show Mum and Henry.'

'I bet there'll be loads of pics on the net,' I said. 'When we get home, we can just Google City Palace in Udaipur and there'll be a ton of stuff on there.'

'You're right,' said Pia and put away her camera. 'I'm just going to relax and enjoy it.'

Over by the lakeside were turrets and domed balconies where you could sit and look out over the water to the mountains beyond. We sat with JJ for a moment to gaze at the view as a group of tourists passed through with their guide.

'Muslin or silk curtains which had been soaked in rose or jasmine water would have been hung across the arched doorways and windows so that, in the heat of the sun, the scent would waft through the rooms,' the guide was telling the group.

'Imagine how romantic that would have been,' I

said to Pia. 'Sitting here with a handsome prince, gazing out at this view.'

'I miss my prince Henry,' she said, then glanced at JJ.

'But we've only been gone two days!' I said.

'Seems like longer,' said Pia. 'Not that I mind but already I feel like we've been away forever and being here, in these stunning locations, well, it'd be nice to have him here too. This place just reeks of romance.'

She winked at me, grabbed Ramesh and pulled him into the next room, leaving JJ and me alone, though I noticed Vanya pause for a moment before he followed Pia.

'It's unreal, isn't it?' JJ said. The view was awesome. We could see the Taj Lake Palace floating in the middle of the water, the hills in the distance.

'It's not what I expected at all. I had no idea India was going to be so beautiful. I mean, I'd seen pictures of the Taj Mahal but this . . . this is like the best decorators in the world got their heads together to make a work of art.'

JJ turned towards me. 'I'm glad you like it,' he said. 'Do you know what I wish, though? That I could see what the people who lived here then looked like. I wish I could travel back in time and see their faces,

look into their eyes. I know there are loads of paintings around but I'd like to see them for real.'

'I know just what you mean. I'd love to know the
stories behind what went on here.'

JJ nodded. 'That's why I love reading the history of
a place, but there's still so much of it that won't have
been written down.'

I nodded and we sat looking out over the view for a
few more minutes, both of us lost in our imaginings of
how it must have been so many years ago. At last we
were alone. I wanted to savour the moment. It was a
magical location, a gentle breeze wafted through the
palace. It was well worth waiting for. Pia had been
right. Romance was in the air. JJ put one hand around
my waist and pulled me closer to him. I felt like we
were the only people in the whole world, caught in a
timeless moment. He put his hand under my chin and
gently lifted it. I closed my eyes ready for his kiss.

'The architecture of the palace is a mixture of
Rajasthani and Mughal styles,' boomed a loud Indian
voice behind us.

I opened my eyes and turned. A tourist group of
about thirty people was standing with their guide,
staring at us as though we were part of the scenery.
One Japanese lady even took a photo of us!

'Seems like we're *never* to get our moment alone,' JJ laughed as he stood up, took my hand and pulled me towards the room where Ramesh, Vanya and Pia had gone.

8
Movie Set

'Dad's playing a big-time jewel thief,' JJ said as we walked through another courtyard in the grounds of the City Palace. 'They shot some of the movie interiors in the Crystal Gallery at the Fateh Prakesh Palace hotel. It's not far. Want to go and take a look?'

'Love to,' I said, but really I thought, *Boring. Traipsing around looking at a bunch of glasses.*

We found the hotel then went up to an upper floor where Alisha came to find us. I liked the Fateh Prakesh Palace. It hadn't been modernised like the hotel we were staying in and it felt like we were stepping back in time to the era of the great maharajas.

It smelt wonderfully of beeswax, probably used to polish the wood-panelled walls.

Alisha was buzzing with excitement about the two boys she'd met.

'Kunal and Prasad,' she said as we made our way down a dark wooden corridor. 'Prasad's the one I like and I think he likes me too.'

'Long distance love affair? Is that a good idea?' asked Pia.

'They're both at school in England, back here for the holidays,' she replied. 'Yay ... Whoa! Wow. Get a load of this!' She stopped and stared around the room we'd just entered. It was full of the most beautiful glassware: bowls, decanters, glasses and mirrors but not just those, there was actual furniture chiselled from crystal: sofas, a bed, a table, a throne and foot-stool, a dressing table.

'They're like exquisite ice sculptures,' I said. 'Imagine the work that went into making them.' Some of the pieces were carved in pale green glass, some in a delicate translucent pink. It was like walking into the white witch's palace in Narnia but this wasn't fantasy, it was reality. As we continued to explore room after room full of glass artefacts, chandeliers and furniture, we were joined by Ramesh who had come with us.

'In these rooms is the largest private collection of

crystal in the world,' said Ramesh, as we paused to look at a vast glass dining table laid with a dinner service for what looked like dozens of guests.

'How old is it?' asked Pia.

'Over one hundred years,' Ramesh replied. 'It was ordered from the F and C Osler company in Birmingham, England by Maharaja Sajjan Singh who began his reign in 1874 but sadly died ten years later. He never got to see it completed.'

'None of it?' I asked.

Ramesh shook his head. 'No, madam, and neither did anyone else. On its arrival in India, it was immediately packed away in boxes underground.'

I looked from JJ to Pia and Alisha. 'Forgotten,' I said, in disbelief. 'But it must be priceless.'

'Yes, madam. It only came to light in recent years and then the head of the Mewar royal family, Shriji Arvind Singh Mewar, decided that this great treasure should be shared with the world and this gallery was opened in 1994.'

'Wow,' said Pia as we looked at a glass wardrobe in one room. 'Imagine finding treasure like this in your basement! How amazing to think this stuff was just packed away in a cellar. It's so beautiful. Each piece is a work of art.'

'This whole place is,' I added.

'Can you buy any of it?' asked Alisha.

Ramesh shook his head. 'No, madam.'

'Shame,' said Alisha. 'I'd love to have that pale pink dressing table.'

'Money can't buy everything, sis,' said JJ. 'It's a real honour for the film crew to be allowed to film here.'

'It is indeed,' said Ramesh. 'And this evening, I believe they will be shooting a scene in the Darbar Hall below.'

We made our way out of the final gallery back into the corridor, from where we could see through scalloped arches into a hall below.

'These would have been the viewing galleries for the royal ladies,' said JJ. 'Isn't that right, Ramesh?'

Ramesh nodded. 'You are correct, sir. Such places are to be found in palaces all over India, often with a lattice screen or silk curtains so the women could stand and observe what was happening in court but not be seen.'

'Cool,' said Alisha. 'A chance to spy on the guys. I like it.'

For a moment, I imagined myself as a princess hundreds of years ago, gazing down at the colourful spectacle in the hall. Chandeliers shaped like giant dewdrops hung from the high ceiling, while portraits, presumably of previous rulers of Udaipur, lined the walls, as well as a display of ancient swords and other weapons.

'It looks like it hasn't changed for centuries,' I said as, in my mind, bejewelled princes lounged about on silk cushions, drinking tea or reading by the light of one of the many antique lamps.

'Apart from all the film equipment,' said JJ.

I followed his gaze and saw that dozens of silver metal boxes of various sizes were stacked on one side of the hall. They contained all the equipment needed to film the next sequence. A team of electricians were busy adjusting lights which hung from a complex arrangement of scaffolding that almost filled one wall. Others were rearranging furniture, hiding cables, adjusting light reflectors and generally making everything ready for the actors. Many of them were speaking into radios or mobile phones.

'It was a banqueting hall, wasn't it?' JJ asked.

'It was, sir,' said Ramesh, 'and today is still used for weddings, meetings and parties.'

'I'd like to get married here,' said Alisha.

'Better find a husband first,' said JJ. 'Typical you. Pick the venue before the man.'

Alisha stuck out her bottom lip. 'Mom and Dad are always telling us that to be a winner in life, you have to be prepared, know what you want and where you're going, yeah?'

JJ scoffed. 'You'd better find a guy first.'

Alisha sighed. 'Yeah. If only. It's not for lack of trying, you know.'

'You're too fussy,' said JJ. 'You want Mr Perfect.'

I gave her arm a squeeze. I knew the fact that she hadn't ever had a boyfriend was a sore point for her.

'But things are looking up since this morning. I really like Prasad,' she said.

'Does he know you're checking out wedding venues already, Miss Fusspot?' asked JJ. 'Jeez, Alisha. You only met him today.'

'You so don't get me, JJ,' she said.

'Tell us more about the movie,' I said, trying to change the subject before they started squabbling.

'Tell us about the boys later,' I heard Pia whisper to Alisha.

Behind JJ's back, I saw Alisha throw a mock punch at him.

'It's a period thriller. Dad plays the part of a Robin Hood type character who robs from the rich to give

106

to the poor. In the case of old India, to the untouchables.'

At the mention of the untouchables, I saw Ramesh's face flash with interest but he didn't say anything.

'They're not shooting a long scene this evening, but it's an important one that links all the others,' said Alisha. 'It's where the Maharaja's daughter spots Dad's character in the palace.'

'Shreya's playing that part, isn't she?' I asked and JJ nodded.

'Who are the untouchables?' asked Pia.

'Haven't you heard of the caste system?' asked JJ.

Pia nodded. 'Yes. It's something like the class system in our country, isn't it, Ramesh?'

Ramesh paused before answering as if carefully considering his words. 'There were four castes,' he told us. 'First the Brahmin caste who were priests and teachers, then the Kshatriyas who were the rulers, warriors and soldiers, next came the Vaisyas, the farmers, workers, merchants and artisans, fourth came the Sudras who were the labourers and unskilled workers.'

'But what about the untouchables?' Pia insisted. 'Where did they fit?'

Ramesh sighed. 'They didn't, madam. The

untouchables were considered the lowest of the low. They were the outcasts of society. For instance, if a Brahmin even accidentally touched one of them, he would have to bathe to remove the pollution.'

'Wow, that's harsh,' said Alisha. 'Sounds as bad or even worse than how slaves were treated back home.'

'And the system's been abolished?' I asked. 'Please say yes.'

'Oh yes. It was abolished by the government in the 1960s, though some say that the roots are so deeply entrenched in Indian history and society that it is still apparent. Mahatma Ghandi did much for the abolition and he renamed the untouchables the children of God.'

'That sounds way better than outcast,' said Pia.

'Seems mad to me,' said JJ. 'I mean, prick anyone's skin and they bleed. Everyone has feelings and every society has good and bad people which is nothing to do with what caste or race they were born into.'

'Exactly,' said Ramesh, 'but in this country, progress is slow. To call anyone an untouchable is now considered wrong, politically incorrect, and in fact, there is a woman who was born an untouchable and is now a respected figure in our parliament. That could never have happened before but it will still take time for the old prejudices to disappear completely.'

'It's a bit like where we live,' I said. 'Some people insist they are working class, others upper. But it's not really about class any more, it's money that's the real divide between the haves and the have nots.'

Pia was looking at me with a strange expression. I glanced at JJ and Alisha and wondered if I shouldn't have said that, but it made me sad to think that some people were seen as outcasts just because of a system they were born into.

It's a mad world, I thought. Back at home, I saw how at Number 1, Porchester Park, the residents were super rich while not a few metres away, sitting outside in a shop doorway, was Eddie, the homeless man who only had a cardboard box to sleep in. People often walked away from him when they saw him asking for money. *Maybe things haven't changed that much*, I thought. I also realised how little I knew about this country I was visiting and vowed to read up about India more when I got home.

'I agree,' said JJ. 'That's why I want to be a lawyer. See what I can give back.' His phone bleeped that he had a message. He glanced at it. 'Shreya,' he said, then grimaced. 'Wants to know where we are.'

'We?' I asked with mock surprise.

JJ pulled a face. 'Jess, I need to talk to you about Shreya.'

My stomach knotted uncomfortably but I didn't let my anxiety show on my face. 'Yes?'

Before he got a chance to say any more, a vision appeared at the end of the corridor. We all did a double-take. Shreya was dressed in her costume for the movie – a ruby-encrusted red silk sari, gold earrings and nose ring, her eyes darkened with kohl. A string of tiny pearls shone in her hair and diamond and gold bangles sparkled on her wrists and ankles. She looked incredible, every inch a princess. It was as if she'd stepped out of one of the ancient family portraits that lined the room. She stopped and posed for a moment, well aware of the impact she was having, then grinned and waved at us all before doing a little twirl.

'Hey,' she called. 'What do you think?'

'Stunning,' I said and I meant it.

She swished her way towards us, her jewels tinkling as she walked. 'I'm ready, so everyone else better had be. You guys going to come and watch?' she asked, but her question was directed at JJ.

Before anyone could answer, Mrs Lewis appeared

behind us. 'Oh, there you all are. Quickly, come with me,' she said. 'The director's found a place we can watch where we'll be out of the way. We're very lucky to be allowed, but you must keep completely silent, so no talking. OK?'

'OK, Mrs Lewis,' I said, then looked at Pia, who mimed zipping her mouth shut.

'See you later. Wish me to break a leg,' said Shreya, misquoting the actor's cliché of wishing each other luck.

I didn't dare correct her. I felt intimidated by her. We all wished her luck and she disappeared back down the corridor, then we said our goodbyes and thanks to Ramesh. I couldn't wait to witness the filming and followed Mrs Lewis down the stairs and into the back of the hall.

We were met by an assistant director who, after speaking into his radio, showed us where to stand.

'The director wants to do this all in one take,' he said. 'Mr Lewis will enter from the far end of the hall. He will run along the side, keeping in the shadows where he will encounter Shreya, the princess, then they will both exit over there.' He pointed to a small door close to us. 'So please, no movement at all while we're shooting.'

We all nodded in agreement, then he spoke into his radio again and was off. I hoped that Pia wouldn't get one of her giggling fits. She often did if we were in places where we knew we mustn't laugh. Nerves probably. Trouble was, it usually set me off too.

I turned to Alisha and, even in the dim light, I could see that she was blushing. Two tall Indian boys had entered the hall and were coming over to join us in our corner. Divinely handsome and clearly brothers, one maybe around eighteen with shoulder-length hair, the other slightly younger with shorter hair. The younger one stepped forward and put his hand out to JJ.

'You must be JJ,' he said. 'We've been looking forward to meeting you. I'm Prasad and this is my brother, Kunal.' He glanced at Alisha, who smiled then tossed her hair in an attempt to look cool.

I glanced at Pia, who raised an eyebrow at me. We didn't need to say anything. Alisha had met her prince.

JJ just had time to quickly introduce Pia and me before there was a shout for silence.

Ignoring it, Kunal stepped close to me and whispered, 'Will you be at the party tomorrow?'

'Hush,' warned the assistant director from a short distance away.

Kunal made a short bow in apology. I glanced at JJ, who had been watching. I couldn't help feeling flattered that Kunal had asked. *Now you know how I feel when Shreya flirts with you, JJ,* I thought. No harm in him seeing that other boys noticed me in the same way that girls noticed him.

At the far end of the hall, I saw Jefferson Lewis and Shreya arrive. They exchanged a few quick words with the director then, to their left, someone called, 'Action'.

There was such a buzz of energy in the room, the atmosphere, the setting, JJ standing next to me – just being there was a thrill. JJ moved closer and took my hand. Double thrill.

Jefferson crept into the hall, keeping his back to the wall. A noise to his right alerted him that someone had come in. He darted back into the shadows. Shreya entered and looked around her. It was really quiet – as if everyone in the room was holding their breath along with Jefferson.

'I know you're here,' Shreya called.

Jefferson shrank back further against the wall.

The hall was completely silent and still as we waited to see what happened next.

'*I tawt I taw a puddy tat a creepin' up on me,*'

sounded the voice of Tweety Pie, shattering the silence.

It was *my* mobile. I'd downloaded the ringtone to my phone before we'd left the UK.

Pia burst out laughing.

I wanted the ground to open up and swallow me. *So* not funny.

'CUT!' called the director as a hundred angry faces turned in my direction.

9
Queen of Deep

'I blew it,' I said the next morning as Pia and I took a break from our studying. 'I *totally* blew it.'

Pia sighed. 'No, you didn't. You saw what happened. They did ten takes in the end. It happens all the time. Planes fly over scenes in historical movies and they have to reshoot, plus Shreya was wearing a watch in the first three takes, for heaven's sake. Somehow I don't think they had Cartier back in the fifteen-hundreds.'

'Yeah, but *I* should have known better.'

'*She* should have known better; she's the movie star, not you. If Prasad hadn't noticed the watch, they might have had to go back to shoot today. I thought they had people on set to notice bloopers like that. What about that microphone in shot on one of the last takes! It's amazing what gets through – there are endless websites showing famous errors like that.'

'I still feel like an idiot.'

'Stop obsessing. Get over it. Everyone makes mistakes and it was cool in the end.'

After the shoot, I'd apologised to everyone I could find, to the director, to Jefferson, to Mrs Lewis, to JJ and Alisha. They were all very sweet about it but I wondered if they had put on polite masks and, as soon as I was out of earshot, they were agreeing that I was a total eejit. I even apologised to Shreya. She hadn't been so sweet and had treated me like I was invisible the rest of the evening. I even overheard her saying to Kunal that the first take would have been the best one if only the stupid English girl hadn't ruined it. And she insisted on introducing JJ to all the film crew so once again, he and I didn't manage to get any time to ourselves. He'd glanced over at me a few times and shrugged as if to say that there wasn't a lot that he could do about it.

'Why doesn't Shreya go for Kunal?' I asked. 'He's from her A-lister world.' Alisha had told us more about the brothers on the way back from the shoot. Apparently they both went to school at Eton in England and were home for the holidays, staying at the five-star hotel their parents owned on the other side of the lake.

'Alisha told me that Shreya dated Kunal for a while last summer, then moved on to the next boy on her list. Alisha thinks she's the kind of girl who likes a challenge,' said Pia.

'Like a female Tom.'

'Sounds like it. Shame he's not here to distract her. Apparently she's desperate to get away for some beach party in Goa after the wrap party. Loads of celebs from Mumbai are going to be there.'

'I heard. I can't wait for her to go. She even asked JJ if he wanted to go with her to Goa after the party, like I don't exist and am not even worth consider-ing!'

'Maybe you should stake your claim and snog him in public,' Pia suggested.

'Mr and Mrs Lewis might not like that,' I said, 'and I'm probably not their favourite person at the moment after my Tweety Pie interruption.'

'Nah. They're chilled.'

'Do you think Shreya knows that it's JJ's birthday later this week?'

'I doubt it. If she did, she'd want to muscle in on the celebration,' said Pia.

'Although if she's like all these others with their private jets, she could probably go to Goa and then come back again. She's probably doing that, in fact. I just hope she goes for long enough so I can get some space alone with JJ at last.'

'Well, I'm not going to tell her it's his birthday,' Pia said. 'I really don't think JJ's interested in her, but if you're really worried, then ask him.'

'But you said I had to be cool and not act needy.'

'Yes, but I can see it's getting to you. I'm certain he'd reassure you.'

A knock at the door five minutes later announced that Alisha had come to visit. She came into the room and frowned when she saw our books.

'It's so boring you have to do that,' she said, then bounced onto my bed. 'Luckily I got all my study done before the trip.'

'We've just about finished for today,' said Pia.

'Good, because I have a plan. Have you ever done meditation?'

I shook my head. 'I tried it once after reading a magazine article but never properly.'

'Me neither,' said Pia, 'but I've always wanted to give it a go.'

'Me too. Loads of my mates are into it over in LA.'

'The ones with gurus?' I asked.

'Yeah,' said Alisha. 'It's supposed to make you feel calm and cool.' She looked at the books again. 'Good for exam stress, apparently. Anyway, I came to tell you that there's some kind of guru convention festival thing happening at one of the temples in Udaipur today. Prasad has invited me. Could be good. My mates back in the States will be so jealous that I can go and meet loads of different kinds of gurus.'

'A bit like an Elvis convention, then?' I asked.

Alisha laughed. 'Something like that. Maybe we could check it out. Learn the meaning of life and all that, as well as get to know Prasad a bit better.'

It was good to see Alisha looking so happy. Meeting Prasad had really given her a lift.

Pia grimaced. 'A *guru* convention? You're not serious?'

'Yes I am,' said Alisha. 'Apparently there are many different types here in India with different takes on the meaning of life. Aren't you into all that what's-it-all-about stuff?'

'No,' said Pia. 'I just get on with living without thinking too much about the whys and wherefores. Are you sure you're not just going along to impress Prasad?'

Alisha feigned offence. 'As if. I'm a *true* seeker.'

'Yeah, of designer handbags,' said Pia.

Alisha picked up a pillow from the bed and playfully threw it at Pia. 'I have hidden depths, you know.'

'Yeah, very well hidden,' said Pia.

'I think about the meaning of life,' I said. 'Often. Especially since my mum died. I questioned everything then, like where have we come from? Where do we go? I spent a long time in the library seeing what different religions had to say about it all.'

'Queen of Deep, that's our Jess,' said Pia.

'And what *did* the books say?' asked Alisha.

I shrugged. 'I only ended up more confused than ever. God, energy, I don't know. I still think about it, a *lot*. Like, here we are on the planet, but what's it all about? Why are we here? *Is* there a God? If religions say that there's one God, why are they always fighting over which one is the one?'

'Exactly,' said Alisha. 'Gurus are supposed to be wise men. I'd like to ask them some of those questions and this afternoon is our chance.'

'Yawn,' said Pia. 'My philosophy is that we humans have a brain the size of a pea, way too small to grasp the mysteries of the cosmos. What we do know, though, is that we're here today, this moment. We don't know when we're going to die so it's best to make the most of it. Enjoy each and every experience that comes your way. Don't waste a minute of it. Especially not by going to guru conventions.'

'I think that's pretty deep,' I said. 'So you're Queen of Deep too.'

'Nah. I'm a simple soul,' said Pia.

'Yeah. I'll back that,' said Alisha and this time, Pia picked up a pillow and bashed her with it.

They were just getting set for a good pillow fight when Alisha's phone bleeped that she had a message. She glanced at the screen. 'Oops, it's Mom. Better go.' She got up to leave. 'Laters. Don't study too hard.' And she was gone.

A short time later, I looked out of the window and saw a speedboat with Alisha, JJ, Mrs Lewis and Vanya whooshing away across the water. I made myself focus back on my books. We'd be joining them soon. I was intrigued by the gurus thing – if we were going to meet some of the wisest people in the world this afternoon then I had a question I'd like to ask. It was a question I'd carried around with me ever since Mum passed away. Where do people go when they die? If any of them could give me a satisfactory answer to that, I'd be well impressed. I couldn't wait to get there and see what they said. Plus, hopefully, JJ and I would be able to slip away and get some time alone. In the meantime, though, I had to clear my head of the mysteries of life and all thoughts of romantic liaisons; I had homework to do.

10

It's Raining Gurus!

'Have you noticed that drivers in this country avoid collisions with their ears as well as their eyes?' I said to Pia as we dodged our way through noisy traffic in Udaipur town. It was early afternoon and we were on our way to meet the Lewises. The streets were a cacophony of hooting from car and truck horns, bicycle bells and mopeds, as drivers and riders wove their way around each other, narrowly missing hitting each other in many cases. So many of the cars had tinsel on the bumpers and most had garlands and small, colourful pictures of gods, gurus or goddesses inside, hanging from the mirror. As I watched the variety of transport going past in all different directions – forwards *and* sideways – I saw that people would toot when they got too close to each other to let them know they were there. In the middle of it all were goats and cows walking serenely by, as much a part of the scenery as the rest of it.

'Toto, I've a feeling we're not in Kansas any more. We must be over the rainbow!' I said as an elephant strolled by, its face and trunk painted in blue chalky patterns, followed soon after by a camel, then a family of white boars.

Pia took a photo on her camera to send back home, then we followed Vanya past a market where women in brightly coloured saris sat in the middle of a pile of open sacks selling fruits, vegetables, spices and herbs. In contrast to the tranquil atmosphere back at our all-white hotel, the town was bursting with life and colour. Some people wore traditional Indian dress, some modern dress, many were tourists in shorts, sarongs and T-shirts. But, as I'd noticed the day before, all life was present as we made our way through the narrow streets lined with open kiosks and stalls. Seated women made garlands from heaps of yellow and orange flowers, old men rested on the pavement, children watched passers-by. Most shops seemed to be geared up for tourists, selling bags, shoes, scarves, tie-dyed bedspreads and clothing, prints of Krishna, goddesses, demons, monkey gods and elephant gods, stone carvings, jewellery and wooden toys. Many of the stallholders beckoned us to 'come and look' but Vanya ushered us on. I also noticed a number of people begging, sitting with their hands outstretched, a bowl in front of them, some old, some only children, running alongside the tourists and tugging at their arms. It made me feel uncomfortable and I wished I could do something to help.

We managed to persuade Vanya to stop at a kiosk selling pashminas. 'Let me demonstrate how you can tell if a shawl is genuine,' said the young stallholder as he held up a ring in one hand then carefully began to thread a large maroon shawl through it. To our amazement, it flowed through the ring like it was the finest silk. As we moved on, I looked over to see a stall selling samosas. 'I'm going to get one,' I said to Pia. 'Want one?'

Vanya held up his hand. 'Not a good idea,' he said. 'Only eat from places you know how the food has been prepared.' He indicated his stomach then pulled a face as if he was ill. We got the message but the smell was so enticing that I bought one anyway. 'It looks fresh,' I said as a smiling Indian man put it in a bag for me. 'I'll have it later,' I said.

Pia fanned her face. 'I'm too hot to eat anything, especially anything spicy.'

Vanya shrugged. 'Don't blame me,' he said as we continued on our way.

'Have you noticed that loads of the signs and posters are in English?' I said as I pointed to a poster advertising a train journey.

'That's because the British were in India for so long,' Pia said. 'From 1612 until 1947. I read about it in one of JJ's books.'

'Clever clogs. You're always so good at remembering dates. I need to read up on it all too. It makes it come to life being here, though, doesn't it? Rather than something you just read.'

Pia nodded. 'Which is why we have to make the most of the time we have out here and not spend it all stuck back at the hotel studying.'

'Exactly,' I agreed, wishing that we'd had longer to browse the stalls before going to the guru convention. I wanted to buy presents for Dad, Gran, Aunt Maddie and Charlie and I still had to buy a birthday present for JJ. But Vanya was a man on a mission and that mission was to get us to the Lewises, leaving us no choice but to hurry along beside him.

'India has such a distinct smell,' I said as we glimpsed the temple ahead of us. 'How would you describe it?'

Pia sniffed the air. 'A mix of ... spices, dust, petrol and baked earth.'

I noticed a cow that was looking at an ice-cream stall with interest. 'And dung, that's definitely mixed in somewhere. There's an animal smell. There are so many oxen around.'

'And goats,' said Pia as she almost fell over one that scurried past.

We went up some steps to an entrance flanked by two life-size stone elephants, then we were at the steps leading to the Jagdish Temple. I could see the Lewises standing in the crowd, amongst a large number of holy men, some in orange robes, some in white, some wearing hardly anything and others looking like they were covered in flour, their faces painted orange, red or blue.

'They look like they've been to a kid's party,' said Pia as we passed one man whose bald head was painted white, with a red stripe down his forehead to his nose and orange cheeks. Around his neck he wore about thirty beaded necklaces. Pia suddenly giggled and nudged me. I looked to my left where there was a bearded man standing totally naked apart from a string of beads around his neck.

'It's a look,' I said. 'Not one that I think will catch on in England though. Bit too cold.'

'Thank God,' said Pia, averting her eyes.

'Wow. This place is amazing,' I said as I took in where we were.

The three-storey temple was stunning, with hundreds of tiny images of gods, goddesses, elephants, dancing girls, musicians, horses and horsemen carved into its pillars.

JJ came forward to meet us. 'The elephants are a symbol of prosperity,' he said, 'the horsemen of power.'

'Why do so many of the carvings have the faces cut out?' I asked when I noticed that lots of the carvings were headless.

'The Moghuls defaced them when they were persecuting the Hindus, because they were of Hindu gods,' said JJ.

I nodded like I knew what he meant and once again wished I'd read up more on India before coming here. I hated feeling so ignorant.

'It must have taken years to carve all these,' said

Pia as we stared at the intricate carvings that seemed to go on forever.

As Pia took photos of the pillars, I noticed that some Indian people were staring at the Lewises with the same interest as we had in the holy men.

'People are staring at you,' I whispered to JJ. 'They must know your dad is Jefferson Lewis.'

'Ah, there's a reason for the looks and it's not because of Dad,' said JJ as we made our way over to Alisha and their mum. 'We get stared at here because of our skin colour. They don't see many Afro-Americans so we're a novelty to them.'

'Bit rude,' I said. One group were actually pointing. They weren't trying to be discreet at all and were openly studying JJ as if he was an alien.

He shrugged. 'You get used to it,' he said. 'Now they're staring at you, too.'

I glanced over and, sure enough, the group were now staring at Pia and me as if they'd never seen anyone like us before in their lives.

'Probably your blue eyes,' said JJ. 'The usual eye colour here is brown.'

'There's a lot to get used to here,' I said. 'Not just the elephants in the street but I've noticed loads of beggars, some of them children.'

Alisha nodded. 'I know. It's upsetting, isn't it?'

I nodded back but didn't say much more. I found the extremes of total luxury and abject poverty hard to get my head around, both here and back in the UK. It didn't make sense that some people had so much and others had so little.

JJ took my hand. 'It's a strange world, isn't it?' he said. 'Like, our family lives in the most amazing places and we have an extraordinary lifestyle that allows us to travel to places like this, while some people have nothing.'

'That's exactly what I was just thinking,' I said.

JJ squeezed my hand. 'That's why we get on. I like that you see what's going on around you on every level. You get the extremes, the contrast in lifestyles.'

'I do and I wish I could do something to help,' I said.

'Me too,' JJ agreed. 'It's hard to know where to start sometimes, though, isn't it? Mom and Dad give a lot to charity, and they both agree that it's important to give something back if you're earning a lot. Like, Mom's donations have helped build a school in the north of India, but sometimes she gets a bit freaked out by the number of requests for help we get. Some from organisations, some from individuals – everyone has their story and so many are in need, but we can't give to everyone.'

'I went to a Christmas dinner for the homeless back in London last December,' I said. 'My Aunt Maddie helped organise it. When I learnt what had happened to some of them, it really changed the way I saw them, so I completely get what you're saying. Everyone has their story. But how do you decide who to give to and who not?'

'Mom has an assistant in LA who deals with all of that. She helps her decide but there are days when both of them get upset. We haven't enough to help everyone and some of the cases are pretty distressing.'

What he said made me think. I sometimes gave some coins to the beggars in London but with my small amount of pocket money, I often felt that there was little I could do to address the imbalance of wealth – and here was JJ whose family were loaded and he felt the same. I was glad to hear that his family helped, though, it made me feel closer to him and less guilty about the amazing luxury we were experiencing travelling with them.

On the next set of steps, Indian women were sitting and making garlands of gold and red flowers for people going into the temple. Mrs Lewis dropped some coins into a basket and gave us each a necklace of flowers to wear.

'This place is awesome,' said Pia as we reached a large brass statue of a half man, half eagle.

To our left, a holy man with white dreadlocks, naked from the waist up, was smoking a pipe. I wrinkled my nose.

JJ sniffed the air. 'Hashish,' he said. 'So the spiritual high isn't totally natural after all!'

Alisha took a look around at the crowd of tourists and assorted holy men, some dressed, some not, and grimaced. 'This is so not what I expected. It's like Crazyville up here.'

'I told you so, sis,' said JJ, then turned to me. 'She really thought we'd be going to some cool LA spa type place where you could buy a bottle of secret elixir or sit in some elegant air-conditioned room and get enlightened as easily as switching on a lightbulb.'

Alisha frowned. 'Apparently there's a guru on every street corner here. How are you supposed to know which ones are genuine?'

'Just look around you, Alisha,' said JJ, and he indicated the many Westerners in the crowd who were dressed in Indian clothes. 'All these people are here to find out which guru is the real thing. So many seekers on a quest. All looking for answers to the big questions.'

Alisha spotted Prasad at the back of the temple and her face lit up. 'Ah, talking of the real thing ... see you later, guys.'

'Don't go too far,' Mrs Lewis warned, then she saw Prasad. 'Stay with him.'

Alisha gave her mother a thumbs-up and disappeared into the crowd.

'Do you want me to follow?' asked Vanya.

Mrs Lewis shook her head. 'I'll keep an eye out for her and maybe you can check on her every now and then too.'

Vanya nodded. Poor Alisha, she wasn't going to get time alone with Prasad, either.

Me, JJ and Pia set off to explore the temple, with Mrs Lewis and Vanya not far behind us. If I'd thought I was on another planet before in Udaipur town, as we went from room to room in the temple I felt like I was in another universe. It was bizarre. In one area, there was a holy man with his right arm held up in the air.

'Apparently he's kept it up like that for four years,' JJ told us.

'Why?' asked Pia.

'Something about overcoming the physical restraints of the body,' said JJ. 'I read about it in a leaflet back at the hotel.'

'But surely we were meant to use our arms,' said Pia. 'So not using them is like going against God. Or like someone cooking a really nice dinner and then their guest saying, "No, ta, I'm going to put it in the bin to show that I don't need to eat it".'

'I guess, but each to his own,' said JJ. 'There are some holy men who stand on one leg for years, and others who fast for months on end. And one man rolled himself all the way to a religious festival, miles and miles away.'

'Rolled?' I asked.

JJ nodded. 'Yeah, he made his body into a roly-poly wheel type thing.'

'Why didn't he just get a bus?' asked Pia.

JJ shrugged.

'And this helps you get enlightened?' I asked. 'Because I don't think Alisha's going to want to do anything like stand on one leg for a year ... There has to be an easier way. And seriously, what's with all the naked guys?'

'Apparently it's the highest form of renunciation,' JJ replied. 'By their nakedness, they're showing that they want nothing of this material world. No rags, no clothes.'

I supposed that kind of made sense, though it was still a bit disconcerting seeing so many beardy naked guys wandering about, however holy they were.

Just then, a group of young Westerners in orange dhotis passed behind us chanting, 'Hare Krishna, Hare Rama.' I couldn't help but smile watching them, they seemed so happy, grinning their heads off and banging their bells and drums like they'd just had the best news ever. I noticed that they had a little tuft of hair at the back of their shaved heads.

'What's that all about?' I asked JJ. 'Did they miss a bit?'

'I heard that they leave it like that so God can pull them up to heaven when he's ready,' said JJ.

'Ouch,' I said. 'Bet that would hurt.'

We turned a corner to see a group of people lining up.

'What's the queue for?' Pia asked a young blonde girl who was waiting in line.

She pointed to a poster of an elderly Indian lady. 'We're waiting to be hugged,' she said.

'OK . . .' said Pia, but she didn't pursue it. The girl had an intense look about her, her eyes slightly glazed, and I got the feeling that Pia didn't want to get pulled in.

'Fancy a hug?' asked JJ.

'From you,' I said. 'Not from some old lady I don't know.'

'*I'll* give you a hug,' said Pia and clasped me to her. 'Feel anything?'

I laughed. 'Yes. A small and very hot English girl. Now get off!'

JJ pulled me over to look at a poster outside a small tent in the corner advertising a laughing workshop. 'Hey, let's check this out,' he said. 'I could do with a laugh.'

We filed into the tent with a few other people. I turned to check if Mrs Lewis was going to join us and saw that Alisha and Prasad were with her. Alisha pulled a face to let me know that the whole convention wasn't her thing. I indicated the workshop poster and Alisha glanced at it then shook her head, so I turned back and joined Pia and JJ.

About twenty of us were crowded into the small tent when an Indian man with a beard and long white hair came in and greeted everyone. 'Welcome, welcome,' he said, beaming as we took our places at the back.

'Everyone ready to laugh?' asked the bearded man.

A few said, 'yes', others shifted about on their feet as if they weren't quite sure.

'First we start with joke,' said the man. 'How many gurus does it take to change a lightbulb?'

Nobody answered.

'None. Change has to come from within.'

There was a little laughter and a groan from the crowd.

'Ah,' said the man with a big grin, 'but see, you smiling now. Smiling good. Laughing better. Best medicine. So. First, we're going to do silent laughing.' He demonstrated someone laughing without sound and I couldn't help but smile while watching him. He looked so funny.

'Now you do the same,' he instructed.

'My speciality,' said Pia and joined in immediately by shaking her shoulders. She was good at it too, having perfected the art of silent laughing in school assemblies.

After a few minutes of everyone laughing silently, the Indian man spoke again. 'And now we do full body laugh.' He began to laugh out loud, then chant, 'I am so happy, I am so relaxed, hahahahahahahaha.'

I glanced at JJ and he shrugged then joined in. 'Hahahaha,' we all chorused.

'LOUDER,' called the teacher.

'HAHAHAHAHAHAHA,' the crowd chorused, so we went for it too and waved our arms in the air as the Indian teacher was doing. It was infectious and, in a few moments, people were genuinely cracking up as they watched each other. At one point, I noticed that Vanya, Mrs Lewis, Prasad and Alisha were standing at the back. They didn't join in. They stood quietly, looking on with bemusement, then left, presumably to try out some other method of finding peace.

'From the belly,' urged the teacher. 'Deep laughing. Ho ho ho ho.'

I glanced over at JJ who was really going for the full body laugh and that made me laugh even more. *Never in my wildest fantasies did I imagine that I'd be out with JJ acting mad like this*, I thought as I threw myself back into it.

'I have to admit I feel good after that,' I said as we left a short time later, 'but I can't say I feel I've gained any insight.'

'You've missed the point then,' said Pia. 'He was

saying laughter is good medicine. Keep smiling. Better than standing on one leg for ten years, don't you think?'

'I guess,' I replied. 'I'll give it a try next time I'm feeling down about something.'

Alisha spotted us coming out of the tent and came to join us. 'I've been meditating,' she said. 'It's not easy. You have to breathe through alternate nostrils and count. You're supposed to let your mind go quiet as you do it but as soon as I close my eyes, a million thoughts are there and my stomach's talking, telling me it wants feeding.'

'How long did you do it for?' asked JJ.

'A couple of minutes.'

JJ rolled his eyes. 'Alisha! It probably takes years to master. You have to give it some time.' He turned to me and Pia. 'Alisha has no patience. She wants everything now.'

'I am *so* misunderstood,' said Alisha. 'It was my idea to come here, you know. Can I help it if I know what works for me? I only need to glance in a shop to know if it's for me or not. And it's the same here. There are some seriously mad people here. Like one sadhu, one of the stark naked ones, had weights through his, um ... dangly bits. Like, *ew*. Excuse me but even *I* know that is not the way to enlighten-ment.'

Pia immediately wanted to go and take a photo but Alisha called her back.

'Don't bother,' said Alisha. 'He's more enlightened than we think. He charges fifty dollars to have his picture taken.'

'What's the difference between a sadhu and a guru?' I asked as Prasad came over.

'A sadhu is a wandering monk,' he explained. 'While guru means teacher. *Gu* means darkness and *ru* means light, so a guru is someone who takes you from darkness into light.'

Alisha smiled at him. 'Now *that* I can understand,' she said. I could see that she had come out of her own darkness and into the light as far as Prasad was concerned.

We spent another half an hour looking around. Amidst the painted and naked sadhus were a number of gurus who had lovely, smiling faces. Most were dressed in white clothes and had bunches of enrap-tured devotees sitting at their feet listening to them. I stopped by one group who were with a guru who was sitting in the lotus position. There was such an aura of peace coming off him that I decided that he'd be the one to speak to, so I sat on the ground with the others.

He looked over at me with brown twinkly eyes. 'You have a question, child?'

I nodded. 'I do. Er ...' I felt myself go red as everyone turned to look at me. 'Where do we go after death?'

'Hmm. Big question,' said the guru and the group around him laughed.

'I know,' I said.

He considered what I'd asked. 'I have to report that the only way to know that is ...' The crowd around him held their breath. '... to die and find out.' The crowd sighed but I'm not sure with admiration at the simplicity of his answer or with disappointment.

'Does *anybody* here know?' I persisted.

'I cannot speak for others,' said the guru, 'but I *can* tell you that you will hear different things. Some will say that after death, you will be reborn again into another body. That is the theory of reincarnation. It is believed that the soul never dies. The body wears out and so the soul, which is immortal, passes from one mortal frame to another in the same way that we cast off one set of clothes and put on another. Others will tell you that this world is unreal, a dream state, an illusion and that when we die, we return and awaken to our true home.'

'So how do you know which is the right answer?' I asked.

The guru bowed to me. 'You must die to find out. In the meantime, you are here. Be here now. Enjoy. Don't waste a minute. Experience where you are.'

'That's what my friend Pia says.'

'This Pia is very wise,' said the guru.

'If reincarnation is true, will we always come back as humans?' I asked, as Pia came to sit with me.

'That depends on karma. Do you know karma?' asked the guru.

'Is it like a chicken dish?' asked an Englishman who was sitting next to me. 'Chicken karma.'

The guru laughed. 'No, my son. That is korma. Also very good. But karma means how you live your life in the present will come back to you in the future. As you sow, so shall you reap.'

'So we'll all be farmers,' said Pia.

The guru cracked up laughing. 'Of a kind,' he said, then he looked at me for a moment. 'Do not dwell on the past. It has gone. Do not waste your life with talk or thoughts about the future. The future is a closed curtain. You must endeavour to be here now, in this present moment, because it is all that is real.'

'How do you be here now in different time zones, guru?' asked the Englishman. 'Like, it's five hours behind in the UK. Should I be here now in India or be there then in the UK?'

The guru looked at him very patiently. 'You are here now. Not in UK. Use your breath to anchor you here. The breath is always here, now. Concentrate on it and it will also bring you peace. Meditate.'

'I like that,' I said to Pia. 'Makes sense.'

We stood up and made a bow of thanks in the way that we had seen others do. We went over to the edge of the temple to wait for Mrs Lewis, JJ and Alisha and, as I stood there looking over the jostling crowd, I tried to focus on my breath. Be here now. I felt like laughing. Be here now in the blazing heat with a couple of hundred people, some of whom looked like they were at a sci-fi convention. JJ spotted me and came over. My fantasies about being alone with him seemed to be getting more and more distant by the minute. I'd always known that we'd be with people some of the time on this trip but never in my wildest dreams did I imagine that we'd be in a crowd of gurus and sadhus, some wise, some naked, some stoned and some clearly out to lunch. Not that I minded that much. It was only day three of our trip and there would be opportunities later to be alone with JJ. In the meantime, it had been an amazing and unexpected afternoon.

'*Om shanti om*, Pia,' I said.

She grinned back. I knew she was feeling the same. '*Om shanti om*, babe.'

11

Rajasthan Rumbles

'Mum says we can have what we like: mani, pedi, facial. We have two hours before the party,' said Alisha when we got back to our hotel.

'I—' I was about to say that I couldn't afford a treatment at the spa. I'd seen the brochure left in our room and even having my nails done was way beyond my budget.

Alisha read my thoughts and waved a hand as if dismissing them. 'You're our guests,' she said. 'Just give your room number.'

'Serious?' asked Pia.

'Serious,' said Alisha.

'*Cool,*' said Pia.

For the next two hours, we had the most divine time. We were massaged, pummelled and exfoliated to within an inch of our life, and our nails were done to perfection – I went for pink, Alisha for dark purple and Pia for bright turquoise with glitter.

'I'm really looking forward to this evening,' I said as we lay on white sunbeds by the pool after our treatments. 'It's the part of the trip I've been looking forward to most. Our first big party with real-life movie stars in one of the most gorgeous locations in the world. It doesn't get *any* better.'

'Mff,' said Pia, as she flicked through *Vogue India*. 'It'll be a party straight out of *Gossip Girl*.'

I stretched out and wiggled my toes. 'Except this is India, not New York. Weird, isn't it? An hour ago we were with hermits who have nothing, not even clothes, and here we are in one of the most luxurious hotels in the world amongst people who have every-thing. Don't you find it hard to get your head around?'

Pia shrugged. 'Not really. I reckon your mum got the balance right. She loved life with all its little lux-uries and pleasures, but she always made sure she put something back, too.'

Pia was right. Mum never talked religion or

questioned the meaning of life. She just got on with it and made sure she did what she could when someone was in need.

JJ was also by the pool sunbathing and reading and when he saw that we'd finished our beauty treatments, he came over to sit on the end of my sunbed. 'Hi, golden girl,' he said and held up a bottle of suncream. 'You've caught the sun today. Want me to do your back?'

Alisha looked up from her magazine. 'Oh, get a room,' she said.

I felt myself blush – more pink girl than golden girl. JJ ignored his sister and indicated that I should sit up and turn around. It felt delicious to have him massage the lotion into my back and, despite the late afternoon heat, his hands sent shivers through me. 'The Indian sun's pretty strong,' he said as he gently kneaded my shoulders. 'Even though there's a breeze, the rays can burn.'

'Just an excuse to get your hands on Jess,' said Alisha.

'And *that* is why I want to have some time alone with you,' JJ whispered. 'My sister is driving me mad. Let's try to slip away for a while tonight while everyone's preoccupied with the party.'

Pia put her magazine aside and sat up. 'Me next,' she said to JJ and pointed at the lotion. I didn't mind. I had a secret rendezvous for later.

'We probably look as mad to those sadhus with their painted faces as they did to us,' I said to Pia as I applied caramel-coloured eye shadow to my eyelids once we were back in our room.

'Maybe we should paint our faces red and orange,' she replied. 'You know, when in Rome, do as the Romans do. When in India, do as the Indians do.'

'Wake up and smell the curry, dozo. Most Indians do not paint their faces bright colours. That's just the sadhus.'

'Spoilsport,' said Pia. 'It'd be one way to stand out in the crowd.'

We already had our outfits for the party because Alisha had insisted that we raid her wardrobe before we left England. It was to be a super-glamorous affair and we knew that our usual sparkly tops were not going to cut it. As I'm the same height as Alisha, choosing my outfit hadn't been difficult and I'd picked a stunning long dress in powder blue silk. It looked plain on the hanger but was cut like a dream. Pia had a harder time finding something because she's so much smaller than me and Alisha, but she borrowed a gorgeous silver halterneck top to wear with a long silver skirt of her own which, put together, looked like a dress.

When we were ready, we Skyped home. Pia had texted earlier in the day to arrange for Charlie and Henry to be together at Charlie's computer. At the allotted time, we rang them and there they were, their familiar faces filling the screen.

Henry let out a wolf-whistle. 'Wow, you two look glam,' he said.

'It's the wrap party tonight,' said Pia. 'What's happening over there? I miss you.'

'Miss you too, babe,' said Henry and he pulled a sad face.

'You're not missing much, though. It's raining outside,' said Charlie. 'We've been hanging out in the VIP shed, playing some music.'

'We?' I asked. I knew that Henry didn't play an instrument.

'Yeah, the boys in the band,' said Charlie.

The VIP shed is at the bottom of our garden. Originally, it held sunloungers for the residents but soon after we'd moved to Porchester Park, Dad let Charlie and me do it up as a den. I had a sudden ache of homesickness. They felt so far away. 'Is Dave around, Chaz?' I asked. 'I miss him so much.'

Charlie disappeared from the screen for a few minutes then reappeared with Dave. He stared at the screen but I wasn't sure he could see me. Some cats can see images on TVs or computers and even themselves in the mirror, but some can't. Gran had a cat that used to watch the wildlife programmes on telly and hop up behind it, as if trying to work out where the animals were.

'Dave, Day-ave,' I said.

He might not have been able to see me but he knew my voice. His ears pricked up and he came right up to the computer screen so that I could see right into his nostrils. 'Dave,' I repeated. 'I miss you. I'll be home soon.'

Dave pawed the screen. '*Meow.*' He looked quizzically at Charlie as if to say, 'What have you done with Jess?'

Charlie laughed and set Dave back down on the floor. 'She'll be home soon.'

Dave wasn't having it, though, and hopped back onto Charlie's knee then stuck his nose in the screen again. 'So, what else has been happening, Chaz?' I asked.

'Flo's been over,' Charlie continued, 'and Tom. He said to say hi and that he misses you, Jess.'

'Yeah, right.'

'She doesn't miss him, do you, Jess?' Pia intervened.

'Actually no, I don't. Not one bit.'

Charlie laughed. 'Probably do his ego some good not to have a girl falling at his feet.'

'Falling at whose feet? Hi, Jess,' said Dad, suddenly appearing behind them. 'How's it going? Got boys falling at your feet, have you?'

'Yes, Dad. Loads of them. It's great here. We love it.' I told them all about the City Palace and the guru convention. Charlie and Henry cracked up when I told them about all the painted, naked men.

'And are Mrs Lewis and Vanya with you all the time?' asked Dad.

'No, Dad. Pia and I have been out partying every night till three, long after the Lewises have gone to bed. No-one minds a bit.'

'Don't joke about, Jess,' said Dad. 'Not when you're so far away.'

Pia appeared over my shoulder. 'We're never left alone, Mr Hall. Don't you worry. And anyway, she has me to look after her.'

'That's what worries me,' said Dad.

'No need, Dad. Vanya or Mrs Lewis are always with us,' I said.

'Good. And you're getting your work done?'

'Every morning. Mrs Lewis is stricter than you are.'

'Good. Take lots of pics. Don't break anyone's heart. See you Saturday – or is it Sunday?' said Dad, then he disappeared.

Typical Dad. Not quite getting what was going on at all.

'I'm off too,' said Charlie. 'Meeting Flo.'

Charlie and Dave disappeared but Henry was still sitting there pulling his sad face. I said goodbye and went out onto the balcony to give him and Pia some time alone. It was amazing, being so far away on the other side of the world but being able to see Dad and Charlie like they were in the same room as us. I wished that they really were. I'd have loved Charlie to have seen all the things I had and Dad needed a break from being on call twenty-four seven. As I looked over the lake, my stomach rumbled and I realised I was hungry. There wasn't time to call room service before we left for the party and I didn't fancy any of the fruit in the bowl in our room. I remembered the samosa that I'd bought earlier in town. I crept into the room and got my bag while Pia chatted away to Henry. I tiptoed back onto the balcony, pulled out the samosa and bit into it. Yummy.

After Pia had finished her call, we went through to reception where there was a group of film people who were staying at the hotel waiting for boats to take them over the lake to the party. Everyone looked like they were dressed up for the Oscars and their various perfumes filled the air. Alisha looked fabulous in a long, figure-hugging red dress with tiny jewels all over it that sparkled when she moved. She was talking to her mum, who looked elegant in steel grey Armani. Jefferson Lewis stood next to them, wearing a simple tailored black suit with Nehru style jacket and grey silk scarf to match his wife's dress. JJ appeared from one of the corridors, immaculate in a cream linen suit. *Real understated style*, I thought, as Pia and I joined them.

'Wow, you look great,' said JJ when he saw me.

I smiled back at him. It was going to be a top night.

Our boat taxis arrived and our group headed off for the Shiv Niwas hotel. JJ sat next to me on the boat. At one point, he took my hand and squeezed it. He gave a sweeping glance to all the people on our boat, then shrugged and smiled. I knew what he was saying: once again we were surrounded by a whole pile of people. But we'd made our promise to each other and I knew that as soon as we could we'd slip away from the party, even if just for a short while.

When we arrived at the hotel, the setting and decoration almost took my breath away. We entered through a tunnel of scented mimosa trees, preceded by dancing girls who cast handfuls of rose petals in our path.

'It must have been like this for the royal families back in the days of the raj,' I whispered to Pia.

'Maybe,' she spluttered. I cracked up. One of the rose petals had flown into her mouth. 'Though I guess you're not meant to eat the flowers.'

The party was being held around the pool area of the hotel and, by the time we got there, most of the guests had already arrived as many of the production people were staying on site. Immediately the Lewis family were swept into the crowd, greeting friends and chatting, leaving Pia and me in a corner. The only person I recognised was the movie's director. I quickly turned my back in case he remembered me and my ringtone.

Pia didn't notice him. She was too busy taking in our location – the illuminated pool, the bougainvillea that cascaded down the surrounding honey-coloured walls, the night jasmine, the pretty table settings. 'It's like a fairytale perfumed garden, isn't it?' she said as she sniffed the air and continued looking around. 'And don't you love the way the burgundy tablecloths match the door and window frames and everywhere else is cream? Great colour combo.' She pulled out her camera. 'Go and stand next to the wall, by that painting,' she instructed, then clicked away as I posed in front of a life-size mural of galloping horses. After that, she made me stand next to another mural of a camel, then in front of an enormous pot that held a full-size palm tree, one of the many positioned around the pool. 'Haha,' she said as she clicked. 'I've made it look as if the plant is growing out of your head.'

'Very artistic,' I said.

'Just one more,' she called. 'Over here.' She led me to an arched, purple doorway. 'Nice backdrop to your dress, now big smile, hold it ...'

As I posed and pouted, Pia was joined by a petite blonde lady who was also holding a camera. 'Are you in the movie?' she asked and took my picture. 'I'm doing a piece for *World* magazine.'

'Oh no,' I said. 'Just friends of the family.'

The lady's face dropped and, without saying anything else, she disappeared off into the crowd.

'Probably off to find someone actually famous,' I said as I looked around at the glamorous crowd who all seemed to know each other. 'I feel like a gatecrasher.'

'Rubbish,' said Pia, as she accepted a glass of juice from a passing waiter. 'We belong here as much as anyone. Don't forget that we're guests of the Lewises. Chill. For all anyone knows, you're the next big teen star. Talking of which ...'

I followed her glance over to where Shreya was making her entrance through an archway on our right. The blonde lady was right there with her camera clicking away as Shreya preened and posed. She looked amazing in a short white cocktail dress, her hair pulled up and back from her face, gold jewellery dripping from her throat and ears.

Pia laughed. 'Now that's how it's done, a real star entrance. We must remember that for going into assembly when we're back at school.'

'Yeah right,' I said. 'I don't know how we'd make our black and white uniform look like vintage Hollywood or, in this case, Bollywood chic.' I watched as Shreya surveyed the crowd as if she was looking for someone. Bingo. She found him and made a beeline for him: JJ. He spotted her, quickly excused himself from the man he was talking to and headed rapidly towards me and Pia. When Shreya saw this, a look of irritation crossed her face.

'Have one of these canapés, they're yummy,' said Pia, who appeared oblivious to Shreya's annoyance on the other side of the pool.

JJ took a canapé then turned to me. 'Want one, Jess?'

I looked at the tray that was being offered and a feeling of queasiness swelled inside me. 'Um, no thanks.'

JJ scrutinised my face. 'You OK? You're looking a little pale.'

'I know. All of a sudden I feel a bit weird. Must have been the boat ride,' I said. 'I never did have sea legs.'

Pia helped herself to another canapé as Alisha, Prasad and Kunal came over. They looked fabulous. Kunal in a coffee-coloured, embroidered Nehru style top and linen trousers, and Prasad in a white silk suit with a white T-shirt and white trainers.

On the other side of the pool, I noticed Jefferson

Lewis chatting to Shreya. A few seconds later, Shreya moved on to talk to someone else then spotted Kunal with us. She beckoned him over to her. I watched as they bent their heads close together then glanced over at me like they were talking about me. *Probably having a laugh about my ringtone ruining the filming,* I thought. I turned my back to show I didn't care what they were saying when Mr Lewis called JJ to join him. JJ went over, then appeared to have an argument with his dad. I saw his jaw clench as Jefferson said something to him. JJ folded his arms as if trying to shut his father out. He glanced over at me, then Shreya drifted back to join them. She was all smiles. *What is going on over there?* I wondered as my stomach churned again. 'Um, Pia. I've just got to go and sit down for a while.'

Kunal appeared at my side. 'Please allow me to escort you,' he said and he took my arm and steered me towards a bench in a quiet alcove.

'Sorry,' I said as I sat down. 'I don't normally – God, I feel weird.'

He took my hand. 'No need to apologise. Can I get you some water?'

I nodded. 'Please.'

On the other side of the pool, I could see that JJ

was still with Shreya. He didn't look happy. She did, though. Kunal returned and handed me a glass of iced water. He touched my cheek gently and said, 'You have a temperature,' just as JJ glanced over at us. A flash of annoyance crossed JJ's face.

'Would you excuse me a moment?' I said to Kunal. I crossed the room, only to see JJ disappear into the crowd to his right. I went in the direction I'd seen him go but couldn't find him. I went a bit further then heard his voice. He was behind one of the enormous palm plants, talking into his phone. 'So, do you get the picture? It's just not working with Jess,' he said. 'I need you out here now to take her off my hands.'

My heart sank. *Oh no. Take me off his hands? Who's he talking to? And what does he mean, it's not working with me?*

I was about to step out and confront him but hesitated. He might think I was snooping. Listening in on anyone's phone calls, especially a boyfriend's, is so not cool.

Suddenly Kunal appeared behind me. 'How are you feeling?' he asked.

'I . . .' Another wave of nausea swelled inside of me. Pinpoints of light flashing off the swimming pool

159

hurt my eyes. Floor tiles with concentric circles at the bottom of the pool in the same burgundy as the tablecloths started to spin. 'Not great.' I had a metallic taste at the back of my mouth. 'I think I need to . . .' I clapped my hand over my mouth.

'Over there,' said Kunal and pointed to a sign that had a painting of an Indian goddess on it. I rushed through the door as fast as I could. Pia came running in after me.

I made it to the loo just in time.

'Whoa!' Pia exclaimed as I puked my guts out.

Moments later, Mrs Lewis burst in, followed by Alisha. I sank to the floor then slid down to lie on the cool marble floor, all dignity forgotten.

'We need to get her back to the hotel,' I heard Mrs Lewis say.

'Can't move,' I groaned. The thought of a boat ride across the lake made my stomach swell again. I knelt up, groaned and crawled to the loo and puked again.

'Oh dear. Alisha, find the manager. Tell him we need a room here,' said Mrs Lewis. 'She can't travel in this condition.'

'Mff,' I agreed. I was in real pain. All I wanted to do was lie down in a dark room. My stomach ached, my head was splitting and my mind was whirling with a blur of images. JJ, Shreya, Kunal. I was aware of someone helping me to my feet, then being walked to a room where I collapsed into a cool bed. I sensed that Pia and Alisha were in the room as I drifted off into a deep sleep. At one point, I opened my eyes to see that a bald Indian doctor had appeared by the bed. He was talking to Mrs Lewis.

'An unfortunate case of Rajasthan rumbles,' he said. 'Sister of Delhi belly and the Jaipur jitters. In plain English, food poisoning.'

'Have you anything she can take?' asked Mrs Lewis.

'I have just the thing,' said the doctor.

It hurt too much to listen or to keep my eyes open, so I closed them again. I felt Pia take my hand.

'Come on, Jess. You have to swallow this tablet,' she said and she lifted my head to drink water and take a pill. 'It will make you feel better.'

I swallowed the bitter-tasting tablet then sank back into the pillows. I felt so weak that even lifting my head had worn me out. 'I'm not going anywhere,' said Pia. 'You just sleep now.'

'I'm here too,' said Alisha.

'Choo,' I said. I meant thank you, but pronouncing the words was too much effort. I let myself drift off.

I couldn't believe it. The one night I'd been looking forward to for ages and JJ was with Shreya while I was alone in a strange hotel room with a devastating dose of the Rajasthan rumbles.

12

The Human Cannonball

'You awake?' asked Pia.

'Umpf,' I said as I attempted to open my eyes. It felt like someone had stuck my eyelids together then clobbered me over the head with a hammer, but at least the feeling of being seasick had gone. 'Wow. Where are we?'

I was in a strange room in a rose pink, curtained four-poster bed. Not the Taj. The events of the previous night came flooding back. 'Oh God. Did anyone see me do the technicolour yawn?'

'Only Alisha and Mrs Lewis. It was quite spectacular. Explosive, in fact. You feeling better?'

'Ish.' I sat up. 'Where are we?'

'Imperial suite at the Shri Niwas. Pretty, isn't it?'

I glanced around. We were in a dome-shaped room painted in shades of green with deep pink curtains and chairs and three borders of lotus flowers stencilled around the top of the walls. 'Yes. Wow. Shame I've slept through it. Did you see JJ last night after my pukeathon?'

Pia shrugged. 'Not really. I left the party with you. I was worried. *Really* worried. He texted to ask if you were OK, though.'

I drank a glass of the water next to the bed and glanced at my watch. It was one o'clock. 'Have I been asleep all this time?'

Pia nodded. 'Yep. Snoring and dribbling.'

'No.'

'Well, snoring.'

'Aw, P. And you stayed with me?'

'Mates,' she replied. 'You'd do the same for me. Mrs Lewis stayed here at the hotel too. She was worried about you and took the room next door. She also had my books delivered. At least you got out of study time. She called a short while ago and said that, if you're up for it, she's booked us in for a healing schmealing trip to some kind of massage centre. Aruyvedic, I think she said. Said it would be just what you need. A few healing herbs and some healing hands.'

'I thought we were going to Jaipur today?'

'No chance,' said Pia. 'You need to chill. JJ and Alisha have gone, though. She called to see how you were too.'

As my head cleared, I had a nagging feeling inside that I'd forgotten something. Or had I had a bad dream? I made myself think back over the previous night. No. Oh *no*. JJ's phone call. I hadn't dreamt it. I quickly filled Pia in on what I'd overheard.

She sighed. 'Oh, Jess. I don't know what's going on there but I do know that Shreya was going on the Jaipur trip this morning.'

'Maybe JJ's left me a message on my mobile. Have you seen it?'

Pia shook her head.

'It was in my bag. I'm sure it was,' I said.

Pia got up to look for it. She found the bag and emptied out the contents. 'Nah. Maybe you dropped it when you ran for the loo. I'll check if it's been handed in at the hotel. Sure you had it with you?'

'I . . .' I wasn't sure of anything. 'Last night's a bit of a blur. Hey. What happened to Goa? Wasn't Shreya supposed to be going there?'

'She was but Alisha said that when Shreya tried to get JJ to go to Goa with her, he turned the tables and talked Shreya out of it and persuaded her to stay.'

'To stay? I'd have thought he'd have been glad to get rid of her.'

'Seems not. Alisha doesn't know what's going on either, apart from the fact that Shreya found out about JJ's birthday bash. I'm so sorry, Jess, but we're mates and I know you'd rather know the truth about what's going on. Whatever happens, I think you need to speak to him. You can use my phone.'

She found her mobile and handed it to me. I was about to text then changed my mind. 'Later,' I said. 'I . . . I don't know what to say yet.' I glanced down at the phone. 'Hey, there's a message from Kunal on here. Two in fact.'

Pia nodded. 'Both for you. He wants to see you later if you're up to it. I think he likes you.'

I laughed. 'Well, if he still wants to see me after the Rajasthan rumbles, he must *really* like me. He was very sweet last night.'

'I think he's got the hots for you.'

'Maybe I *should* see him later,' I said. 'He's kind, he's handsome and it will show JJ that if he's going to mess me around, I can play the same game.'

Pia frowned. 'JJ doesn't strike me as someone who plays games.'

'That's what I used to think until I heard him saying that it wasn't working with us. Now I'm beginning to think that the reason we never got any time alone together was because secretly he wanted it that way. I wonder when he changed his mind about wanting me along on the trip? On the plane? When my mobile went off at the movie shoot? When he saw Shreya? Maybe he's realised I don't belong in his world.'

'No way, Jess. You really have to get over being so down on yourself. We've been through this before: just because his family have money doesn't mean that we're excluded because we don't. OK, yeah, some people with dosh might think like that, but I really don't think JJ does. He's bigger than that.'

'Maybe. But something's going on with him and it all started to go weird when Shreya came on the scene. There's something he's not telling me.'

'Perhaps. Just don't do anything impulsive until you hear his side of things, Jess. Rule whatever number we're up to in the relationship guide book is: don't ever assume you know what's going on in your other half's head.'

'I *heard* him, Pia. I didn't make that up or imagine it.'

'Fair enough but … be careful with Kunal,' said Pia. 'Alisha said that out of the two brothers, he's the player. Bit flash, you know. You don't want to do anything stupid with him and blow it with JJ.'

'I guess,' I said. 'I don't know, Pia. This trip is so not turning out how I expected, not on any level.'

'Try not to think about it too much,' said Pia. 'We can text Alisha later and find out what's going on.'

I grimaced. 'That's a hard one. JJ's her brother so she won't want to tell tales on him. I wouldn't want to spy on Charlie.'

'Yes but I don't think she's that keen on Shreya and you're her mate. I'm sure she'll keep us posted. And in the meantime, go with the flow, that's what I think. Let's try and enjoy what time we have here, OK? So, if you can, get out of bed and let's hit the aruyvedic centre.'

I nodded. I didn't want to ruin Pia's time by being miserable. All the same, I had a sinking feeling inside when I thought of JJ travelling with Shreya, exploring new, exciting locations when it should have been me with him. 'Bring it on,' I said as I got out of bed, tripped over a cushion on the floor and bashed my head on a chair.

'You OK?' asked Pia, as I rubbed my forehead.

'Ouch. Yes. No. I don't know.'

Pia laughed. 'Yes, no, don't know? Hmm, that's clear. Really, Jess, you've got to stop drinking first thing in the morning.'

I held out my palm. 'Talk to the hand. The head is concussed.'

'No difference there, then,' said Pia.

'Huh. The sympathy didn't last long. You'd make a rubbish nurse.'

After a light lunch of toast and plain yoghurt for me, vegetable curry and dahl for Pia, Mrs Lewis came to collect us and we drove out to the healing centre by the lake.

'I'm looking forward to trying this place and I've seen Jaipur so it's no sacrifice,' said Mrs Lewis after I'd apologised for the hundredth time for my epic throwing up. 'Now, how are you feeling?'

'Bit weak still but much better, thank you,' I replied as our driver parked outside the centre surrounded by gardens. It was such a relief to be feeling normal again apart from a slight headache.

The thought of a relaxing treatment was very welcome.

A young bearded Indian man in traditional white clothes came out to meet us and ushered us along a veranda into a cool, dark wooden reception where he gave us brochures listing the various treatments on offer.

'Mmm,' said Mrs Lewis as she inhaled the potent herbal scent that permeated the building. 'I feel good already.'

'It's rosemary,' I said. I recognised the smell from Gran's garden.

Mrs Lewis and Pia opted for a facial and after Mrs Lewis had explained to the man behind the desk about my Rajasthan rumbles, it was decided that I should have the detoxifying and reviving full body treatment.

'Sounds great,' I said. A soothing massage with scented oils would soon put me right again. Perfect.

Minutes later, three smiling Indian ladies in red sarongs came to collect us then led us through a maze of dark corridors to the treatment rooms. Mine was at the corner of the building where a brown leather massage table was waiting on a veranda that opened into the garden. My masseuse told me that her name was Sushila and handed me what looked like a plastic nappy.

'Everything off,' she instructed, 'put this on, then lie on couch.'

She left me alone and I looked around for a changing room but there didn't seem to be one so I slipped off my clothes, put on the nappy thing and lay face down on the couch.

Pia stuck her face round the door and cracked up laughing. 'I'm just next door. Mmm, sexy. Want me to take a photo to put on Facebook?'

I clasped my hands to my chest. 'No way. You dare!'

Pia grinned. 'Later,' she said, then disappeared.

Sushila came back a few minutes later with a younger companion who she introduced as Usha. She put on a CD and the sound of someone chanting the word *Om* over and over again filled the area. As I lay on the couch, they poured what seemed like a litre of oil on me then both of them started massaging. Up and down, and up and down. Then the pummelling turned to light slapping.

'*Ommmmmmmmmmmmmmmmmmmmmmmm,*' chanted the voices on the CD, getting deeper ever second. '*A-ommmmmmmm.*'

'Is good for blood and circulation,' said Sushila as she whacked my thighs. 'Rosemary oil. Mmm. Breathe deep. Cleansing.'

As they continued the four-handed massage, the oil was seeping onto the couch, making it more slippery. Pummel, whackity whack, slap. I tried to relax but I felt myself sliding back and forth along the couch in rhythm to their actions. Their movements became faster, so fast that I had to grip on to the side of the couch for dear life because the thrust behind the masseuses' pummelling was causing me to slip forward precariously. *Oh whoa. Any minute now, I'm going to go flying off this couch and into the garden, like a human cannonball.* I dug my fingers into the couch and hung on.

'Relax, *relax*,' urged Sushila. 'You very, *very* tense.'

Yes, because I'm going to shoot off into the flowerbed at any moment, I thought.

'I'm sliding off,' I tried to protest.

Usha nodded. 'Oil. Is good, yes?' she said and continued thwacking and slapping.

When Usha asked me to turn over, I tried to sit up but slid back onto my back with a thwump, trying to hang on to my plastic nappy saturated in oil at the same time.

As I tried to regain my balance and turn over with some dignity, I noticed we were not alone. Three female gardeners in orange saris were leaning on their rakes watching, like I was the afternoon's entertainment. I probably was. One of them waved. 'Nice treatment, yes?'

'*Nooo*,' I wanted to call back. And it wasn't over yet. After they'd finished slapping me about, the two masseuses marched me over to an open air shower and began to wash me down with freezing cold water, like I was a dog who'd got muddy in the park. 'No, no. I can do it myself, honestly,' I begged as I gasped for breath at the shock of the water.

'No, no, we do,' said Usha. 'You relax.'

Are you mad? No way can I relax, I thought. *I'm freezing. I'm naked. I've got goose-pimples. I'm dripping with rosemary oil and I smell like a leg of lamb. Add a few roast potatoes and I'd make the perfect Sunday lunch.*

They clearly didn't sense my discomfort because they continued scrubbing at me with rough flannels. 'Very good for skin,' said Usha.

I gave up and let them do their worst.

After I'd got dressed, I met Mrs Lewis and Pia back in reception. They were both glowing with relaxation after their facials.

'Good treatment?' asked Mrs Lewis. 'Revitalising?'

'Um. It certainly woke me up,' I said. I didn't want to seem ungrateful by saying that I would have paid the masseuses to stop and the best part was the sublime relief I felt when the treatment was finally over.

Mrs Lewis went to settle our bill and I was just about to tell Pia all about the massage when her phone rang.

'Alisha,' she mouthed as she took the call then put it on speaker so that I could hear as well.

'Jaipur is awesome. There's this place called the Red Fort here and it's out of this world. We went up to it on elephants. It was so cool. Shame you missed it. Hey, are you all healed and holy now?'

'Fab facial,' said Pia. 'Jess is being quiet about hers.'

'Oily is a word I could use,' I said.

'What, like Spanish?' she asked.

'No, *oily* not *olé*.'

Alisha laughed. 'Whatever.'

'Is Shreya there with you?' I asked.

Alisha was quiet a beat too long before she replied and my heart sank. 'Yes. And Kunal and Prasad. Um. About Shreya. JJ's . . . Hey, just a sec, the guys are back. Er . . . listen, got to go. Meet us at the landing place for the Taj at . . . what time, JJ?'

'Five,' JJ's voice called. 'Are you talking to Pia?'

'Yeah,' I heard Alisha say.

'Don't let Jess know anything.'

Alisha's phone suddenly clicked off.

Too late, I thought as Pia glanced at me in sympathy.

13

Rescue

'I'm not going,' I said later that afternoon when a taxi boat arrived at the hotel to take us over the lake.

Pia put her fingers into the L for loser sign and held it up to her forehead. 'Planet Loserville, population: you. You can't give in this easily. No. You have to dress in your most lovely clothes, get out there and show JJ what he's missing.'

I wish I had Pia's attitude sometimes but I don't and all I wanted to do was hide in our hotel room and listen to tragic songs about unrequited love while gazing wistfully out over the lake. I can do the Queen of Tragedy act well if I try. Like some of the sad ladies in the Pre-Raphaelite paintings I've seen in books at Gran's – the Lady of Shalott or Ophelia. They adopt a noble, dignified pose that hides a broken heart – except in Ophelia's case where it's not so much dignified as floating dead in a river with soggy weeds in her hair. I'm not that much of a headcase. And maybe tragedy queen is more of an English thing to do on a grey day. Here, the late afternoon sun was sparkling on the lake and I'd already lost half the day being ill then tortured by sadistic masseuses. It seemed mad to be in such a glorious location and miss it because a boy was doing my head in.

I'd found my phone when we got back to the hotel and there were three messages from JJ on it. The last one said he needed to talk to me about Shreya. Well, I didn't want to talk to him about her. Pia was right. I shouldn't give in to Loserville. Alisha had said that Kunal was with them. He liked me, he was fun and he wanted to see me. I'd show JJ that I didn't need him. Course I didn't. I'd be the new Jess Hall. Independent. Irresistible. More ass-kicking Lara Croft than droopy 'I give up on life' Ophelia.

'OK, I'll come with you. I am so over JJ. And if

Kunal is into me, I might just have a holiday romance after all.' I said the words but Pia didn't look convinced.

Neither was I.

'There they are,' said Pia, as our boat drew up at the jetty.

'Don't worry, I've seen them,' I said, 'though I can't see JJ or Shreya.' I'd spotted Alisha, Prasad and Kunal from halfway across the lake. Standing by the shore, they looked like they'd stepped out of the pages of *Teen Vogue*, effortlessly glamorous with their glossy black hair, pale linen clothes and designer shades. I fixed a smile on my face ready to be Miss Happy. I didn't give a damn.

Pia sighed. 'Relax, Jess.'

'I am. Can't you see I'm smiling?'

'No, I can't,' said Pia. 'You look like the Joker in *Batman*. Be yourself. *Relax*.'

'If another person tells me to relax today, I may have to kill them,' I said and mock throttled her. 'I'm trying to do what that happy guru man said. *Make yourself smile and a real smile will follow. Act happy and you will be happy.*'

Pia grimaced. 'I think his philosophy may be

flawed,' she said, 'if you also feel the need to strangle your best mate.'

'Sorry, P. I wish I had a fairy godmother who would make Shreya just go away and everything all right with JJ, but that's not going to happen, is it? He's not even here with the others.'

'Pray to the great fairy godmother in the sky,' said Pia. 'Maybe she'll rustle up a miracle. And why are we being so sexist? Why not a fairy godfather or god-brother even?'

'True. Or a guardian angel. I used to think I had one when I was little and she'd watch over me at night with her wings spread out over the top of the bed. I used to move over to make room for her because I thought she might be tired standing there all night.'

'Do you still believe in guardian angels?'

I shook my head. 'If I have one, these days she has a bad case of PMT.'

Pia laughed. 'Fairies and angels aside, let's make the best of it. We're in this great place, we look good and the night is young.'

We did look good. Pia had on a bright turquoise halterneck dress that suited her perfectly and I'd made a big effort with my appearance and put on a sweet pink and primrose floral dress. I'd blowdried my hair until it shone. My plan was that JJ would be bowled over and as jealous as hell when he saw me flirting with Kunal.

Small setback in the plan, though. No JJ.

Alisha spotted our boat arriving and waved. I waved back and we soon joined her, Vanya and the handsome brothers on the shore.

'How are you feeling?' asked Kunal, his face full of concern.

'Happy. Oh so happy,' I said and gave him a big smile.

He and Pia looked at me as if I was mad.

'It's the drugs they gave her,' said Pia and pointed at her head as if to say I'd lost the plot. 'Where are JJ and the teen queen?'

Alisha looked down at her feet and wouldn't look me in the eye. 'Um. Not supposed to say.' She glanced up, shrugged and put her hand on my arm. 'You'll find out later.'

'Why shouldn't she know? I'm sure Shreya said something about wanting to show him the Monsoon Palace,' Kunal said, and pointed to a castle in the distance, on top of a hill on the other side of the lake.

'A beautiful place to watch the sunset,' said Prasad.

'It was built to watch the monsoon clouds and the views from up there are spectacular.'

'It looks so romantic,' said Pia, then clapped her hand to her mouth. She realised that was the last thing I'd want to hear when JJ was off there with Shreya. 'I mean, I thought he wanted us to meet him here.'

'He did. He does,' said Alisha.

Prasad shook his head. 'Sadly he hasn't been getting much say about anything today. Shreya sure is one control freak. And JJ's been acting oddly all day, don't you think? All twitchy and looking at his watch the whole time.'

Alisha pulled me aside. 'Sorry, Jess, I tried to find out more but the only time I got him alone was for a few minutes, and when I asked him what was going on, he tapped his nose like he had some great secret. If Shreya is that secret, I am so going to kill him. But I wouldn't be too worried. They will be chaperoned. Shreya always has to have someone with her, just like we do.'

Prasad pointed back up to the mountains. 'The palace was used as a hunting lodge by the royal family in the past.'

'Perfect,' I said. *The perfect place for Shreya the manhunter to take her latest prey.*

Kunal took my hand. 'But tonight is your night, Jess. To make up for upset.' He rubbed his stomach and flashed me a smile. 'What would you like to do?'

Push Shreya into the lake came to mind but I quickly deleted the thought. 'I don't know,' I replied. 'I, we, don't know the area. Maybe you could tell us?'

'Town is still very busy with all the visitors and holy men from the festival,' said Prasad.

'I'm guru-ed out,' said Alisha. 'So let's pass on town.'

Kunal shot his brother a look. 'What do you girls do when you're at home? To chill out?'

'Have sleepovers. Watch DVDs. Get takeaways. The usual stuff,' said Pia.

'Sounds perfect,' said Kunal. 'Come back to our place and we'll hang out. We can get something from the hotel kitchen then watch some TV.'

Pia pulled me aside. 'Hey, I'm starting to feel like a gooseberry here, you know. You and Kunal, Alisha and Prasad. Do you want me to split?'

'No way. It's not Kunal and me,' I said. 'He's a laugh, yes, but I'm not going to get involved with him.' I linked arms with her and pulled her back towards the others.

We travelled in two taxis to the brothers' family

home in the grounds of their hotel on the other side of the lake. Vanya went in one with Prasad and Alisha, even though Alisha tried her hardest to persuade him that he wasn't needed. He wasn't having any of it and got into the back of the car and sat between her and Prasad. Poor Alisha. She'd finally met a boy she liked and now couldn't get any time alone with him. I knew exactly how *that* felt. Pia, Kunal and I travelled in the other car with Kunal in the middle. His thigh pressed gently against mine as we set off. I moved away and squidged up towards the door and stared out of the window at the passing scenery. My plan had been to flirt with Kunal if JJ had been around to witness it, but in his absence I didn't want Kunal getting any ideas.

No doubt about it, the view was beautiful with the sun setting over the hills. Udaipur was the city of romance and JJ was up a mountain with another girl. We hadn't had five minutes alone together since our first morning here and it was getting more and more unlikely that we ever would, now that Shreya had got her hooks into him.

As we drove on, my thoughts turned to home. I wondered what Dad and Charlie were doing. I had so much to tell them and thought about how I'd describe it all. My Tweety Pie ringtone going off in the middle of the movie shoot, getting the Rajasthan rumbles, then being slapped about by the masseuses and almost flying off the couch into the flowerbeds. Mum would have laughed until she'd cried.

Part of me still thinks about telling her stuff, even though it's over a year since she died. Sometimes I catch myself reaching for my phone and thinking, *must tell Mum that*, or *I wonder what Mum will say about this*, then I have to remind myself that she isn't here. I miss her so much and wished I could call her and tell her all about JJ and what was going on out here. She'd have known how best to deal with it. I remember what she said when she was told that her cancer was terminal and there was nothing more the doctors could do to save her; when she found out that her whole life was not working out as planned. 'You have to be like a tree,' she said, a few days after the news had sunk in, 'it bends in the wind. Resist and stand too stiff and it will break you. The only way to be is to bend with it.' She was still mobile then and started messing about, dancing like a tree in the kitchen, waving her arms around. She acted really daft sometimes.

My eyes filled with sudden tears. Just when I think

I'm over crying about her, the loss of her springs out like a tiger from the bushes and catches me by surprise. She'd been amazing right up until the end. She'd had so many plans. So many things she'd wanted to do but had to let them all go when her life took such an unexpected turn. 'I'm going to make the most of every day, every hour,' she said after she'd shed her angry tears, 'and in that time, I'm going to do my best to find some happiness in this strange situation I've been thrust into.'

That's what I have to do, I decided, although what was happening to me wasn't frightening or sad, like it had been for her. She wouldn't want me to be miserable just because things weren't going the way I wanted. *Let go*, I told myself. *I'm still in this glorious location. Having the trip of a lifetime. I'm with mates. OK, so maybe things haven't worked out with JJ but, just like Mum, I'm going to do my best to find some happiness here. Not the happy-clappy guru's way by laughing like a mad girl, but by being grounded and making the best of things. And like a blooming tree, I'm going to bend in the wind of change.*

Prasad and Kunal lived with their parents in a spacious bungalow. Unlike the heritage hotels, this place looked like something from a futuristic movie, with spotless black marble floors in the high-ceilinged central reception area where the restaurants were and honey-coloured guest bungalows with verandas dotted around the grounds. We had a fun evening with the boys and they really made us laugh.

'We're going to have an Eeenglish,' said Prasad, putting on a strong Indian accent.

'Make mine really bland,' said Kunal, joining in with his brother in his exaggerated accent. 'Go strong on the ketchup. I can take it.'

Pia and I cracked up. I knew the comedy sketch that they were quoting. I'd seen it on telly back home; it was a skit about a group of English-born Indians parodying us Brits when we order an Indian takeaway and compete as to who can take the spiciest.

Our supper wasn't bland at all. The hotel had an Italian chef so we had pasta. It was delicious and actually a nice change from the spicy food we'd been eating for the last few days.

After supper, Kunal showed us his collection of DVDs. He had a wall full of English and American sitcoms.

'*Fawlty Towers* is my favourite. And my dad's. He

roars with laughter at Basil Fawlty,' he said as we settled down to watch an episode.

After the meal and DVD, Pia talked about Henry and how she missed him. Prasad insisted that she Skype him from the super-duper computer in their business centre as it had a huge screen, so they disappeared off with Alisha. Vanya had gone to have supper in the hotel restaurant so that left Kunal and me alone.

Alone at last, but with the wrong boy, I thought, as he put on a DVD of *The Office* (another of his favourite English sitcoms). He sat back on the sofa and rolled up what I thought was a cigarette. As soon as he started smoking, I recognised the smell from the temple steps earlier in the week. Hashish. He inhaled deeply then offered me the joint.

I shook my head.

'It's OK,' said Kunal. 'I won't tell.'

'It's not that. I don't smoke dope.'

'I thought everyone smoked over in English schools.'

I laughed. 'No way. I mean, yeah, some people do but not me. Thanks.'

'Have you ever tried it?'

'No.'

'Then how do you know it's not for you?'

'I . . .' I wasn't sure what to say or how to handle the situation. He probably thought I was really uncool for refusing a smoke, but I knew people at school who smoked and didn't like how it affected them. We called them dopeheads, because that's exactly how they acted: dopey. A mate of Charlie's had had to leave school and go to hospital for six months for mental health problems after smoking skunk. I wouldn't be able to tell which was the lighter type of dope and which was skunk so I wasn't going to risk it. 'I prefer to be clear-headed,' I said, 'that's all.'

I'd made up my mind ages ago to be like that, after Josh Tyler had tried to pressurise me into smoking it at one party, making out that I was acting like a scared kid if I didn't. I almost gave in because I didn't want to appear childish. Pia and I had had a long talk about it at the time and decided that actually it was more immature to give in and do something we didn't want to just because some people might say we were uncool.

Kunal just shrugged and we continued watching TV for a while. He snuggled over and got cosy, which I didn't mind. We were just a couple of mates hanging out, weren't we? A cuddle was OK. But then he slipped his hand into mine and entwined his fingers with mine. Still OK but I'm not totally stupid. I knew boys rarely did cuddles if they didn't want more. Kunal started playing with my fingers, caressing them. It was definitely feeling like he wanted to be more than mates. He moved in, nuzzling my neck and beginning to kiss me.

I wasn't sure what to do. To give in or push him off. But then I thought, *JJ is probably snogging Shreya up at the Monsoon Palace right now. Yeah. Stuff him*, I thought and I stopped resisting and kissed Kunal back.

He moved closer, pushed me back into the cushions and moved so that he was half on top of me. He gently traced my profile with his fingers. Actually, it felt nice. I hadn't had that much experience with boys and it was interesting how different it felt being with him to being with JJ or Tom. His breathing began to get slightly faster and the hand that was tracing my face began to move lower. 'I really like you, Jess,' he whispered, as he nibbled my ear. His hand began to stray down to my chest. I moved it off. He moved it back. I moved it off. He sat back. 'Aren't you into this?'

'I . . .' I wasn't sure how to react. As with the dope

smoking, I didn't want to be pressurised into anything that I didn't want to do. 'Yes. And I like you too, but we've just met. Can't we slow things down a bit?'

Kunal sighed. 'I guess. Just you're so hot, Jess, and you'll be going home soon.' He snuggled in again. 'See? I can't resist you. You're like a magnet to me.'

I laughed and he took it as a sign to start kissing me again. I kissed him back and once again, his hand began to stray. This time onto my leg and under my skirt. He was about to start moving it up my thigh when I pushed him off again. 'I *mean* it, Kunal.'

He sat up again and sighed heavily. 'But why not? We're attracted to each other. What's wrong?'

I wasn't going to be argued into going further than I wanted. I felt confused and hot, and not hot in the way that Kunal meant. I was supposed to be with JJ on this trip, not with some strange boy I'd only just met, no matter how handsome or charming he was. Suddenly I had a great idea.

'Hey, I know what we can do.'

'What?'

'You like massage?'

Kunal nodded. 'Yeah.'

'I can do aruyvedic.'

Kunal raised an eyebrow. 'Really?'

'Yes. Take your shirt off, lie on the floor and I'll massage you.'

'Don't we need oil?'

'If you have some,' I said.

Kunal quickly fetched some oil from the bathroom and a pile of fluffy towels which he laid out on the rug. I kept my face straight because I knew he thought he was in for a sensual, lovely time. He whipped his clothes off down to his boxers and lay face-down on the towels.

'This is a great idea, Jess,' he said as I dripped oil onto him then started gently massaging his shoulders. 'Ooo,' he groaned softly. 'Hey, you're good at this. Keep going, a bit lower.'

I began slapping, lightly at first, then stronger.

'Hey! Ow!' Kunal cried. 'What do you think you're doing?'

'Ayurvedic. It's good for the blood,' I said. 'Now relax, relax, you're very tense.'

'Are you sure it's meant to hurt?' asked Kunal.

'Absolutely. I had a treatment myself this morning. Good for the circulation.' I had to stop myself laughing out loud. If nothing else, it had cooled his ardour. I continued with the slapping when suddenly he pushed himself up onto his elbows. 'Um. Maybe massage isn't your thing after all, Jess. Can't you go back to the nice, gentle part, like when you started?'

'OK,' I said. 'Lie back down. I'll try another method.' I remembered Mum having a shiatsu massage once and the therapist had used her elbows to give a good strong pressure. I knelt beside Kunal and stuck my elbow into his shoulder and leaned in on it.

'Ye-OW!' said Kunal. 'That *really* hurt.'

I shook my head. 'So much tension there, that's why you have to breathe into it.'

Kunal sat up and pulled one of the towels around him. 'I think I'll leave it for now, thanks,' he said, as the door opened and Pia, Alisha and Prasad came back in. They looked surprised to see Kunal half dressed on the floor.

'What's been going on here?' asked Alisha.

'Massage, aruyvedic style, and a bit of shiatsu,' I said. 'Sadly Kunal doesn't like it.'

Pia cracked up. She knew exactly what I'd been up to because I'd told her all about my massage from hell earlier.

'JJ texted that he's coming over to join us,' said Alisha. 'He'll be here in a sec.'

'Just JJ?' I asked.

Alisha glanced at Pia and gave her a sly smile. There was something going on. 'No,' she said. 'He has someone with him.'

A knock alerted us to the arrival of JJ. He came in and looked startled to see Kunal just in his boxers and me kneeling next to him. Shreya came tripping in beside him. I turned towards Kunal and pretended to laugh at something he'd said, like it was the funniest thing ever. I glanced back at JJ. Hah. That showed him. He looked well annoyed.

'Just a moment,' said JJ. 'I need to speak to Jess.' He beckoned me outside so I got up and followed him out onto the veranda. 'I've been texting you all day. You didn't reply. And what's been going on back there?' He indicated the bungalow.

'Oh, we were just hanging out with the boys,' I said. I wasn't sure what to say. I felt confused, and now that I was face to face with JJ, my game plan of using Kunal to make him feel jealous felt wrong. I made myself remember that he had been off somewhere with Shreya.

'I left my phone at the hotel, but I got your messages earlier. You wanted to talk about Shreya? Someone said you'd been up to some palace in the mountains with her.'

Now it was JJ's turn to be confused. 'Mountains? What mountains?'

'Kunal said he thought you'd gone to the Monsoon Palace with her.'

A flash of irritation crossed JJ's face. 'He did, did he? Well, I can tell you I wasn't up a mountain with Shreya.'

'So where were you?'

'I was ... Hey, Jess, what's going on here? Did anything happen with you and Kunal in there? And are you OK after the other night?'

'I ... I've never been better,' I said, and glanced back in the direction of the room where the others were. 'Kunal's been ... er, very kind to me.'

JJ's expression had turned to stone. 'I *bet* he has,' he said. 'Jess, I really think we need to talk.'

I knew what that meant. Everyone does. After the 'We need to talk' line comes the 'Can we still be friends?' line. Basically meaning, it's over. I was finding it hard to think straight. My whole plan had backfired. So not how I'd imagined it would be with him. 'About Shreya. Listen, JJ, it's fine. I mean it wasn't but ... I did some thinking and I don't own you. And it's not like we've been going out for ages, so fine. You go ahead with her. I ... I'm cool.'

He reached out and grasped my hand. 'Go ahead with Shreya? No! What are you talking about?'

Oh God, I have got this so totally wrong, I thought as I looked into his face. He looked as upset as I felt.

'Last night, I . . . I heard you say on your phone that things weren't working out and you wanted me off your hands, though I wish you'd told me yourself—'

'Off my hands?' He looked confused, then his expression changed, as though he'd suddenly realised something. 'No! Not *you*. God. I would have explained everything if you hadn't thrown up, then Mum wouldn't let me in to see you and you haven't been answering my texts. Listen—'

Shreya opened the door behind us. 'Come on, JJ. Alexei wanted us to order food for him.'

'Alexei?'

'Hey, Jess,' said a familiar voice.

It can't be, I thought, as I turned around but there he was coming through the gardens towards us.

'No way!' I said and went over to give him a hug. 'What are you *doing* here?'

Alexei flashed a look at JJ. 'Man on a mission. JJ called, begging me to rescue him. Hasn't he told you?'

'Rescue him?'

'I've been trying—' JJ started.

'Said he couldn't get any time with you so needed me to take a certain somebody off his hands.'

I glanced at JJ. 'Shreya?'

JJ nodded. *That's* what I meant by it wasn't working with you. Not that it wasn't *working* working – but that we could never get any time alone. Shreya did this whole number on my dad saying how lonely she was and how she needed friends and that she could really relate to me. Dad said that I had to keep Shreya sweet and keep her company, which meant you and I could never hang out. Also Dad didn't want Shreya disappearing off to Goa in case there had to be any reshoots on the movie. I'd been getting all these texts from Alexei about how bored he was in Paris and how he was ready to fly over if he was welcome, so it gave me an idea – and it seems to be working. Shreya came with me to the airport, took one look at Alexei and—'

Alexei bowed. 'Happy to help out,' he said with a grin. 'But I'm starving. Let's eat!'

Oh my God, I thought as the penny dropped. *Oh my God. I have been so stupid. And I let Kunal kiss me and I kissed him back. What if JJ finds out? It's me who hasn't been trustworthy, not JJ.*

'JJ, I've been such an idiot,' I said. 'I ...' I glanced in the direction of the bungalow.

'Vot's going on?' asked Alexei.

'Misunderstanding,' I said. 'Big misunderstanding.' I turned to JJ. 'I'm so sorry I didn't trust you.' He still had hold of my hand. I squeezed it. 'Really sorry. I thought you wanted to be with Shreya.'

JJ laughed. 'No way. Hence our man here. He's been longing to join us and now here he is.'

Alexei rubbed his stomach. 'Hey. Didn't someone say something about food?'

JJ pointed at the door. 'In there,' he said and Alexei headed in to join the others.

I started to laugh.

'What's so funny?' asked JJ.

'Alexei,' I said. 'I prayed for a fairy godbrother and he turned up after all.'

'So, are we OK?' asked JJ.

I nodded. 'Er ... about Kunal ...'

'You like him?'

'No *way*. It's you I want to be with. And what about Shreya?'

JJ laughed. 'A drama queen and a control freak. I don't think so. She is *so* not my type. It's *you* I want to be with.'

I still felt guilty about having kissed Kunal and wondered whether to tell JJ. I so didn't want to blow it with him and was torn between being totally honest and a fear that if he knew about the kiss, he'd dump me. 'I . . . I . . .'

'We want to be with each other and no-one's going to get in the way,' said JJ, as if picking up on my thoughts. 'So, let's forget about Shreya and Kunal. Enough said about them. Deal?'

'Deal,' I agreed, heaving an inward sigh of relief.

14

JJ's Birthday

Our remaining days were a blur of temples, palaces and beautiful hotels where we stopped for lunch or tea. JJ's plan worked like a dream. Shreya totally fell for Alexei and when they weren't out with us, they were off on their own somewhere comparing watches or the designer clothes and gadgets that they were both so into. It was a match made in heaven. At last JJ was free and his dad was happy that Shreya had company. The only trouble was that, as the week went on, and Alisha and Prasad got more loved up, and Alexei went off with Shreya, it became more and more evident that Pia was the only one not in a couple.

'You can go out with JJ if you want,' she said.

'No way,' I said. 'Mates come first, always. Anyway, you know we can't go too far unaccompanied. I can see JJ when we're back in the UK.' I meant it too. Now that I knew that JJ and I were OK with each other and that he wasn't into Shreya, I didn't mind so much that we were chaperoned on all the excursions we went on. I'd let go of my expectations and fantasies of being alone with him in romantic locations and had come to accept that for this trip, we were always going to be with other people. If not Mr and Mrs Lewis, then Vanya would be somewhere keeping an eye on us and if he wasn't around, then Alisha, Pia and Prasad were. Since the night that Alexei arrived, Kunal had kept his distance. Alisha told me that Prasad had confided in her that on the night of the wrap party, Shreya had asked Kunal to keep me out of the way so that she could be with JJ. When I heard that, I was so glad I'd given him my version of an ayurvedic massage. I only wished I'd slapped him harder. I couldn't stay mad for long, though. There was too much to see, too much to take in and enjoy. After the awe we'd felt at the A-list lifestyle at the beginning of the trip, Pia and I had taken to it like ducks to water and were loving every single second.

On the last day, for JJ's birthday, our whole group – the Lewis family, Prasad, Vanya, Pia and I – travelled in three vintage Bentleys to the Deogarh Mahal, a hotel about an hour from Udaipur. It was a vast terracotta-coloured palace built in the seventeenth century and spread out on top of a hill. It looked like Disney meets Bollywood with its turrets, domes, terraces and balconies. I texted Charlie and told him to Google it so that he could see exactly where we were. He texted back half an hour later. **Awesome. Looks like an amazing fort. Curry on, party girl. C U l8r. Chaz**

Lunch was served up on a terrace on top of the palace from where it seemed like we could see the whole of India stretched out before us – a breathtaking panorama of hills, lakes and mountains in the distance. While we ate plates of fresh mango, we watched a beautiful young girl, in a red traditional dress, balance four wicker baskets on her head while she danced barefoot on broken glass. It didn't seem to hurt but I did wonder about her life. She looked around the same age as me but our lives were so different.

'Maybe she's the Indian Lady Gaga,' Pia commented.

After lunch, we meandered down the hill into the

town of Deogarh, where Mr and Mrs Lewis browsed the stalls and bought bits and pieces from the stall-holders. Mr Lewis kept his shades on but no-one appeared to recognise him and he seemed to relish moving about anonymously for a change. I was amazed at what I was able to buy with the money I had: pashminas for Gran and Aunt Maddie, silver bracelets for Flo and Meg, a small drum for Charlie, a painting of an elephant on silk for Dad's office. Everything was so affordable and Pia was a dab hand at bargaining, something we soon found out was expected and part of the fun.

'But what can I get for JJ?' I asked Alisha as we looked at a stall selling silk paintings. I had to find something because we'd all agreed that we'd give him our gifts at the birthday dinner on the barge that evening.

'I know. Difficult one,' she said. 'He's got watches, clothes and he even got a car last year.'

I laughed. 'A car's a bit out of my budget. What have you got him?'

'I usually get him fun stuff, you know, to make him laugh. Like a jokey book or a DVD. But from you, maybe something personal, like, can you draw or paint?'

'Not brilliantly.'

'Or write? Maybe you could write him a story or a poem. Something like that. I think that's what he'd treasure. Something money can't buy.'

'Yes, but what?'

'You'll think of something,' she said, then went to catch up with Prasad who had gone ahead and was looking at a stall selling old books.

I glanced at the stalls lined up ahead along the street and saw that a lot of them were selling bric-a-brac and antiques. Some of it was junk but there were some nice pieces, though nothing that seemed right for JJ. At one stall, I noticed that there was a box underneath the table full of old photos. 'Can I look?' I asked the stallholder.

He nodded. 'Yes. Look, look.'

I knelt down and flicked through the photos. They were very old. Most were black and white, some were sepia, some faded and a little torn around the edges. They showed various family groups sitting in palaces that looked very similar to some of the ones we'd visited. In one, the man of the family sat on a throne by a pillar. He had a big moustache, was dressed in a jewelled and embroidered tunic with a sash and had a silk turban on his head. He was looking down his nose at the camera, his expression wonderfully haughty. Behind him, two male servants in white traditional dress stood to attention, while at his feet sat a sulky teenage girl, her left hand pulling her sari over her hair and face as if she didn't want to be photographed. Another photo showed a group of men sitting on the steps of what looked like the Deogarh Mahal. Some had long beards and wore tunics with sashes and cummerbunds and were holding weapons similar to the ones we'd seen in the Darber Hall in the City Palace. Everything about them, from their posture to their dress, was regal. Two women in the picture sat at their feet, frowning out from under their saris.

'Where are these photos from?' I asked the stallholder.

'Royal houses. Palaces,' he replied. 'Royal family.'

Pia came over to join me and knelt down to see what I was looking at. I glanced to check that the others had gone on ahead then handed a couple to her.

'I think I've found JJ's birthday present,' I said. 'He told me one day when we were going around City Palace that he wished he could see what the people who lived there looked like. Not just paintings but their real faces. And here they are.'

'Brilliant. Great idea. These are wonderful,' said Pia as she looked at the photos. 'And this one tells a story.' She handed me a sepia photo of an Indian lady on a chair. She was dressed like Shreya had been for the part of the Maharaja's daughter. She looked very majestic and she didn't have the cowed look of the women sitting on the floor in the other photo. This lady was clearly somebody important. By her side stood a young boy of about six years old, his arm resting on her knee; he was dressed in Western safari clothes, even a small pith helmet. 'It shows two eras in Indian history, doesn't it? The lady in traditional dress representing old India, her son representing what was to come with the British raj.'

'How much for the photos?' I asked.

'Two thousand rupees,' said the seller.

'How much is that?' I asked Pia, who was better at working the exchange out than I was.

'About thirty pounds,' she said. 'How much have you got?'

I counted my money. 'About one and a half thousand,' I said. 'Not enough.'

Pia pointed at the three photos I wanted. 'You can do for less?' she asked but the stallholder shook his head.

'Very valuable. Original. No do cheaper.'

Pia got her purse out. 'You have to get these,' she said and she handed me five hundred rupees. 'They're the perfect present.'

I gave her a hug. 'I'll pay you back,' I said as I got up and handed over the money.

In the evening, Pia and I packed our bags before the party so we'd be ready for the early morning flight the next day. I felt I had so many things I wanted to remember from the trip. Snapshots in my mind of the people, the bright sunshine colours, the animals, the stunning locations – like the Ladies' Garden just outside Udaipur where four fountains had been built to sound like rain falling; Lake Pichola, where we took a boat ride; a hotel courtyard strewn with fairy lights where we had dinner one evening, sipping tea as musicians sat nearby playing sitar and tabla, the shops and stalls in the bazaar, where we stopped to watch travelling Kathakari dancers, who looked like Hindu gods come to life – and lastly, the insane traffic and terrifying rickshaw rides with Pia, JJ, Alisha and me stuffed in the back, hanging on for dear life. All separate moments making up a colourful collage in my brain.

'You OK tonight? You're not going to throw up again, are you?' asked Pia as we got into our party clothes.

'I'm thinking of doing it at every celebration,' I replied. 'Like my party trick. See how far I can reach.'

Pia pulled a face. 'Ew. You're disgusting.'

'I try to be,' I said, as I sprayed perfume on my wrists, then headed for the door.

15

Home Sweet Home

I gazed out at the wet London afternoon as we sped along the M4 in the back of the Lewises' UK limo. It felt good to be back in England, even if it was grey and dismal. I was longing to see Dave and Dad and Charlie – though it had only been six days, it felt like we'd been away much longer.

When we arrived back at Porchester Park, the Mercedes pulled up out front and Yoram came over to open the back doors. He looked like he'd sucked a lemon when he realised that he was letting me and Pia out, but when he saw Mrs Lewis and JJ and Alisha, his expression turned to a smile. Yoram had never been friendly to me and Pia. To the residents, however, he was impeccably polite, greeting them with charm and professionalism.

'Back to reality,' Pia whispered. We'd got so used to being part of the in-crowd, it was going to be hard to be just normal again.

We said our goodbyes and thanked Mrs Lewis again for having invited us, then made our way into reception.

'I'll call you later,' said JJ, after he'd given me a hug.

'The parting of the ways,' Pia commented as we crossed over to the door leading to the staff area and the Lewises went to the lift to take them up to their apartment.

'I know. Do you think it's going to be weird going back to our life after having lived in the lap of luxury?' I asked.

'Only if you make it weird,' said Pia and tapped her head. 'It's all in the mind, in your attitude.'

I did a small bow to her. 'You are indeed wise, O small one,' I said. She came out with extraordinary stuff sometimes.

'I know,' said Pia. 'Just call me Guru Pianand ji.'

'Pianand?'

Pia nodded. 'And I'd like you to walk two steps behind me as a sign of respect from now on.'

'Dream on, nutjob,' I said.

Once in the staff area, we went our separate ways and soon I was swept up into my own personal homecoming. A big hug from Dad, a small hug from Charlie – he didn't really do hugs but I could tell he'd missed me – and a good lick and nuzzle from Dave, who didn't hold back in letting me know how glad he was that I was back.

After I'd given my presents out and had a cup of tea and piece of toast with Marmite, I went and sat in my room and looked at my emails. There weren't that many because I'd kept up with them in India and also on the plane coming home, though we'd mainly slept on the return trip. I sent messages to Meg and Flo to let them know we were back, then sat and stared out of the window. It looked so dull outside compared to the bright light of India and it felt like life had suddenly come to an almighty and abrupt full stop. Only the night before, I'd been dressed in my best clothes having dinner by candlelight on the Imperial Barge on Lake Pichola, one of the most beautiful locations in the world. It had been a wonderful evening and JJ had loved his Indian photographs. His favourite present, he told me, which was saying something seeing as his mum and dad had got him a whole hoard of expensive goodies. And now I was back home, looking out of the window at a brick wall opposite.

I got out my phone and texted Pia. **Strange to be back.**

She phoned straight away. 'Yeah. Feels so quiet and Mum won't play the servant game. I told her that I was used to being waited on hand and foot and being served the finest food on the best crockery and that I wanted to be known as Princess Pia from now on. She laughed then threw a tea towel at me, pointed at the sink and said, "Get over it, Lady Muck. Life is all about balance. Now get drying those dishes." I've only been back half an hour and already she's using me as her personal slave.'

'My mum used to say that was one of the perks of having kids,' I said.

'Got to go,' said Pia. 'Mum's calling. Probably wants me to mop the floors. Oh how the mighty are fallen.'

I sat back on my bed and my phone bleeped that I had two texts. The first was from JJ. **Don't want it 2 end yet. Can I C U l8r? Maybe finally get some time alone? XXX**

And the second from Tom. **When can I see you?**
Missed U. Tom XXX

'Tom!' I said to Dave. 'What does *he* want?'

Dave rolled onto his back and pawed the air.

'Yes, he probably wants his tummy tickling too.'
However, after India and Shreya and Kunal, I wasn't
going to mess JJ around, not for a second. We'd had a
good heart-to-heart on the plane coming back, before
we all slept like zombies, and we agreed to be totally up
front about everything from now on. 'So, sorry, Tom.
You might be Mr Cutest-Boy-In-School but you're history.' I meant it too. JJ was my first real relationship
and I wasn't going to blow it by keeping my options
open in case anything went wrong. I trusted JJ and I
didn't feel quite the relationship newbie that I had
when we'd first set out on the trip. I'd learnt a big
lesson – never to assume that you know what is going
on in your boyfriend's head. Never second-guess and
always give him a chance to explain. I'd been off on a
total fantasy in my head about him and Shreya and
almost blown it, all because of my own insecurity.

I texted Tom back. **C U in school. Can't C U b4, too
busy with JJ. Curry on. Jess.**

Next I texted JJ. **Come down as soon as U can.
Bring baseball cap. Have an idea. Jess XX**

I unpacked my bag and went into Charlie's room. He'd gone out but luckily he'd left what I wanted hanging on the back of his door. It was a distinctive green hoodie with rows of white skulls that he'd got from Camden Market.

A ring at the bell downstairs a short time later told me that JJ had arrived. I grabbed the hoodie and went down to let him in. 'I got it,' I called to Dad who was sitting at the breakfast bar having a cup of coffee. 'S'probably just Pia. Popping over there now.'

Dad waved and nodded as if to say OK.

JJ stood at the door when I opened it, Vanya hovering in the background. I quickly put a finger up to my mouth to warn him not to say anything, grabbed my jacket and a couple of umbrellas, then shut the front door behind me so that Dad didn't see that it wasn't Pia. 'We'll look after him,' I called to Vanya. 'Just going to Pia's.'

Vanya nodded. 'Call me when you want to go back up,' he said.

'Will do,' said JJ, and we watched him disappear back down the corridor leading to the reception area. 'Honestly, like anyone's going to abduct me on the premises!'

I handed him the hoodie. 'Ah, but we're not going

to be on the premises. Put this on,' I s▨
cap.'

'Why?' asked JJ.

'It's Charlie's. All the staff will have seen him
going out in it. He wears it most days.'

JJ caught on immediately, put on the hoodie and
pulled the hood over his head. 'Where are we going?'

'To be on our own,' I said and pulled him towards
the staff gate. 'Don't turn around, keep your head
down. If you see anyone, put an umbrella up.'

'But it's stopped raining.'

'Only for a while. It'll probably start again.'

We made our way to the gate and were just about
to exit when Pia's mum, Mrs Carlsen, appeared
behind us. 'Jess, hi. Hi, Charlie.'

JJ immediately put up an umbrella and didn't look
around. 'Mff,' he said.

'Where you off to?' asked Mrs Carlsen.

'Um. Shops. Milk.'

She waved an envelope at me. 'Could you post this
letter for me?'

'Sure,' I said and ran over to get it from her. She
glanced at JJ as I took it from her. 'Charlie OK?'

'Yeah. Good.'

JJ waved his arm without turning around.

Pia's mum rolled her eyes. 'Teenagers,' she said, then thankfully went back inside.

'Phew, that was close,' I said as I opened the gate and we slipped through onto the pavement outside. I punched the air. 'Free!'

JJ put the umbrella back down but he kept the hoodie pulled well over his face and walked close to the wall. 'Let's move it in case anyone sees us.'

I looked back, Yoram was out front in his usual position. I gave him a wave. He saw me but didn't wave back. We walked round a corner then were out of sight.

'You can look up now,' I said to JJ. 'No-one's following us.'

As we made our way down the street, I noticed a newsagent's and it gave me an idea.

'Just wait here a moment,' I said. 'I've got to get something.'

JJ stayed outside while I dashed inside. I returned to him a few minutes later and handed him my purchase. 'A late birthday present to go with the photos,' I said.

His face lit up when he saw that it was a packet of jelly beans. 'My second best present,' he said as he opened it up and popped two in his mouth.

Munching happily, we made our way to the park

where we looked for a quiet spot but it app—
whole world was out enjoying the reprieve betwee—
showers. People were rollerskating and jogging,
mothers were pushing prams, pensioners strolling,
families having picnics, and there were benches full
of businessmen grabbing a sandwich for lunch.

I sighed. 'God, this is worse than India.' I looked
up at the sky. 'And it looks like it's going to pour
again.' Just at that moment, there was a crack of
thunder and the rain started to lash down. Everyone
in the vicinity dashed for the nearest shelter.

JJ and I put up our umbrellas, looked at each other,
then at the people now crammed into the nearest
wooden pavilion. JJ shrugged and indicated a bench
to our left under a tree. He pulled me towards it and
we sat down. He positioned our umbrellas so that
they made a makeshift tent.

'Sorry. I thought there might be somewhere we could
be alone,' I said as I drew my knees up out of the rain.

JJ did the same with his knees then grinned. 'No
problem. Actually it's cosy in here.' It was too. Both
umbrellas were big ones that Dad had brought back
from a posh polo lunch he'd been invited to. The
two together made a pale lilac bubble, cutting us off
from the rest of the world.

'Different from India, hey? Here we are squashed on an uncomfortable old bench in the pouring rain. Not exactly romantic Udaipur, is it?'

I laughed as we heard the rain beat down more intensely, and saw it splashing up from the ground.

'No rose petals, no sun on our faces ...' said JJ, and then he stopped and took a deep breath. We were sitting directly opposite each other, squashed up together. He looked right at me and for a few seconds neither of us moved. We just stared into each other's eyes. The atmosphere inside our small waterproof dome felt charged with electricity. 'Hey. We're finally alone,' he said.

'We are.' I started to laugh.

'What's so funny?' asked JJ.

'It's pouring with rain, our jeans are wet from the bench, we're in this tiny space with no view ...'

'Jelly beans instead of the finest cuisine.'

'And I can't think of a more romantic place to be.'

'Me neither,' said JJ, then looked into my eyes again, then down at my mouth. 'It's amazing in here, isn't it?' he said and, at the same time, we leant towards each other. A kiss at last.

If you enjoy the Million Dollar Mates series,
you'll love Cathy's new book,
Love at Second Sight.
Here's an extract!

'I hold that when a person dies his soul returns again to earth; arrayed in some new flesh guise another mother gives him birth.' John Masefield, *A Creed*

It all started on the May bank holiday weekend.

It was Friday afternoon and I trooped out of school with my best mates, Effy and Tash. Despite the grey skies and threatening rain, they were in a sunny mood, unlike me.

'Three whole days off to hang out with Dave,' said Tash.

'Three whole days to hang out with Mark,' said Effy.

Three whole days for me to be Miss Tag Along, I thought as they talked over plans on the way to the bus stop. It was the second bank holiday of the month and, once again, I'd be the odd one out. Bridget Jones singing, *All by myself.*

'Oh, and to hang out with you too, Jo,' Effy added. 'We wouldn't leave you out.'

I tried to look enthusiastic. I knew I'd be included in any plans. They're good friends and we all know the rules when dating boys: mates come first. Even so, it isn't a ton of fun going to the movies, all five of us, with me wedged in between two couples, not knowing where to look when they snog each other's faces off. Then going for pizza and watching them feed pepperoni to each other across the table while I sip my diet coke and try not to look like a sad loser. Or spending evenings in each other's houses, listening to music, while Mark and Effy or Dave and Tash send slow smiles between them across the room, as if to say 'don't we have something special here?' While I, feeling left out, wonder what I'm doing to put boys off and whether there's something wrong with me because my relationships don't last.

So, no. Another weekend of being reminded that I'm single is not my ideal, that's for sure. Not that I haven't had boyfriends. I have. I've even made a list of them in my diary to remind myself that I'm not a total reject.

My love life so far
By Jo Harris

Jamie
He was back in Year Eleven. I liked him a lot until a small problem came up. He was also dating Cheryl Wilson from Year Ten.

Doug

Also in Year Eleven. He was good company but as time went on, I realised that I paid for everything. Basically he was a cheapskate. I don't get that much pocket money and I thought it would be nice if he bought the cinema tickets once in a while, because it wasn't as if he didn't have any money, he just chose to spend it on CDs or computer games.

Lawrence

He was at the beginning of the Lower Sixth. He could be interesting and funny but was a bit of a dope-head. We didn't last long because I got bored of watching his eyes glaze over and listening to the rubbish he spouted when he was stoned.

Finn O'Brady

I should really cross him off. He belongs more on a wish list than as part of my love life so far. I know he's a total waste of time because loads of people fancy him and I doubt he even knows that I exist. He's lead singer of a band called Minted and is as cute as hell, with girls lining up for him. I met him when Effy and I signed up to be part of a local team putting together a magazine for six schools around the North London area. Finn's in the Upper Sixth at a school down the road from ours and he's the editor. The magazine is called *Chillaxin*. So far, although I've been to two of the meetings, I don't think he even knows my name.

And that was the whole list, apart from Owen, so, all in all, my love life so far has left me with a feeling that boys just do your head in.

Owen is the exception. He's Effy's older brother and we were a couple for a while, for a few months in fact, but he always felt more like my brother than my boyfriend. He's a nice guy, very grown-up and protective. 'You're perfect for each other,' everyone said. 'So many shared interests. *So* alike.' And they were right. We could talk for hours about books and music, the world and how we were going to change it. We *did* have a lot in common, but someone who's the same as me isn't really what I want. Kissing Owen was like eating plain yoghurt. Good for you, but bland. And he used to have a shiny spot on the end of his nose which, though I know it was shallow of me, I couldn't help but focus on whenever he puckered up and moved in. I just thought, ew, pass me the Clearasil. Not exactly how I imagined true love's kiss to be.

OK, so maybe a relationship isn't going to be like a Disney movie, with a heart formation of bluebirds tweeting away in the background, but surely it isn't too much to ask for someone colourful and exciting? And scorching hot. I want someone who'll burst into my life like a flame and challenge me. Make me think. Turn my insides to liquid honey and make my toes curl. Though that sounds like a case of E.coli. What I mean is, I want to *feel* something. A pull. A longing. *Desire*. I want Heathcliff from *Wuthering Heights*, wild and passionate. Or maybe not . . . He was a nutter with mad hair and obsessed with Cathy's ghost. Someone like him would be way too high maintenance as a boyfriend. Who else sounds right? Edward from *Twilight* – the most dangerous and charismatic boy in the school? OK, maybe not him, either. Someone who drinks blood for kicks is probably not the most suitable guy and, anyway, vampires are so last decade. I just want Finn O'Brady.

No. *No*. I will not waste time on someone who has a line of girls after him. What would I be? Number sixteen? Seventeen? One hundred? Oh, I don't know. No, I *do* know. I want to meet my soul-mate. I want to meet a boy who makes me feel alive like I've never felt before and who feels the same way about me – but I'm not convinced that's going to happen where I live in North London. Most of the local boys (apart from Finn) wear those falling-down jeans that show their bum cracks and Calvin Kleins. So not sexy, at least in my book.

'I think I may stay in and catch up with some study,' I said, as the girls discussed going to a movie.

'No way!' said Effy. 'Why don't you want to come with us?'

I shrugged.

'Because you're a singleton?'

'Ish. Look, I'm cool with it. You guys go. Have a good time.'

'You don't need to be single, Jo. You could have boyfriends,' said Tash. 'Loads of boys fancy you.' She pulled her red beret out of her rucksack, put it on and tucked her hair up into it. Her real name's Anastasia, but we call her Tash. She has shoulder-length, titian-red hair that goes frizzy in the damp weather. 'Bane of my life,' she always says. She carries her beret everywhere in case of showers, which is a shame because I think her hair suits her curly. No-one's ever happy, though. Effy has long, silky blonde hair and she curses about it being so fine. My hair's dark, dead straight, and half way down my back and I'd love to have Tash's waves, whereas she's jealous of me and Effy being able to just 'wash and go' without battling with the GHDs.

'Yeah. You're way too picky when it comes to boys,' agreed Effy.

'I just don't want to compromise, that's all.'

'I don't think you should, either,' said Tash. 'I think you should wait for the One.'

'Oh, get real. I mean, we all want to meet the One,' said Effy, 'but until you do, you should get some experience. We're only seventeen. Practise your snogging!'

And so it went on as we waited for the bus. Same old Friday conversation. Same ole, same ole. It's not that Effy and Tash aren't romantic. They are. Way more so than me, in fact. Out of the three of us, I'm the one with my feet most firmly on the ground. I'd like to do journalism, which means thinking rationally, researching ideas, getting facts. Tash and Effy do art and literature so are encouraged to live in the realm of imagination and dreams. I'm right brain, they're left. Effy is an Aries and, even though I'm not as into astrology as she is, I can see that she's typical of the sign and rushes into things at full speed with great enthusiasm. Tash is a Pisces, the sensitive dreamer, and I'm Taurus. Stubborn, says Effy. I prefer to focus on the other qualities, like being loyal, practical and sensual. Whatever the explanation, we're different, but our friendship seems to work despite that. Effy is also a giggler. It's one of her most endearing qualities. It's so easy to make her laugh. Ever since I met her back in junior school, Effy has cracked up at the most inopportune moments, in assembly for example, when Mrs Burton, our headmistress, says something about stealing in the cloakroom or we have a guest speaker talking about their passion for a cause and we're all supposed to be focused and taking it seriously. Effy's shoulders will start shaking with silent laugher. She tries to hold it in but usually fails. And that tends to set me and Tash off too so we all end up in detention for being giddy. Effy's also endlessly curious. As well as astrology, she's into clairvoyants, tarot cards, visualisations and anything alternative. Miss New Age Nutjob, I call her. My mum's into all that stuff too. She and Effy get on like a house of on fire. Most times, I just switch off from both of them when they start ranting on about life and all its mysteries.

Effy glanced at a poster on the wall by the bus stop. 'Hey, look. The fair's coming to the Heath this week-end. Tell you what, let's go on Sunday afternoon. The boys are playing footie, then meeting up with mates afterwards, so it would just be us. We could go to the fair, have some girlie time, win a few teddy bears then head back to yours, Jo, for a sleepover. You in?'

I knew Mum was working late on Sunday night so it was either the fair and a sleepover or staying home alone. 'Sounds like a plan,' I said. 'I'm in.'

By Sunday, the rain had gone and it was a glorious sunny afternoon by the time we made our way over the Heath to the fair. The good weather had brought out the crowds and the atmosphere was buzzing. Effy spotted the clairvoyant's tent almost immediately. She was like a bee to honey. She linked arms with me and pulled me over to read the small sign tacked out-side. *Betty – Past-life readings, Tarot cards and Palmistry.*

'Ten quid to have your fortune told. Come on,' said Effy. 'Maybe she'll tell you if there are any boys in your future.'

I rolled my eyes. 'I bet she tells everyone there's a tall dark stranger on the horizon. Honestly, Ef, you don't really believe in all that rubbish, do you?' I don't know why I asked. Of course she did. She was always consulting the cards, the runes, the I Ching or the stars. Last month, she did my horoscope for me on-line. She wasn't happy when I said that if I met a boy it would be because I'd made an effort to get out there, not because Venus was in conjunction with the moon or whatever. 'Oh, don't be a cynic,' said Effy. 'It's only a bit of fun. *Pleeease*.'

'Yeah, come on, Jo. Let's give her a try,' said Tash. 'Our neighbour, Mrs Adeline, said there was a clairvoyant here last year who was brill.'

'Waste of time,' I said. 'I can think of way better things to spend my money on.'

'Then it's on me,' said Effy. 'An early birthday present.'

I didn't want to appear ungrateful or hurt her feelings, but I'd really rather have some bath products or a CD . . . still, I eventually gave in.

Effy went first and came out fifteen minutes later. 'She's good,' she said. 'You're next and I've paid for you.'

I looked at Tash. 'No, you go next,' I said. 'I insist.'

'Chicken,' said Tash, but she went in all the same.

'So. What did she say?' I asked Effy as we waited.

She shook her head. 'I'll tell you when Tash comes out. We'll compare notes. I don't want to put anything into your head.'

'So it was rubbish, then?'

'No. No. Um . . . nothing that specific, though. I'll tell you later.'

She went and bought us two candyfloss sticks and refused to be budged any further. Ten minutes later, Tash came out with a big smile on her face.

'Don't say anything,' said Effy. 'Not til Jo's been in. Off you go.'

I took a deep breath and entered the tent. It was dark inside and smelled of sandalwood from a joss stick that was burning in the corner. A middle-aged lady was sitting at a small fold-up table which had a crystal ball and a deck of cards on it. She didn't *look* like a clairvoyant. She looked ordinary, with short grey hair, a ruddy complexion and a boring outfit of blue shirt, floral skirt and sandals.

She glanced up at me. 'Jo?'

I nodded.

'Sit,' she instructed and indicated I should take the seat opposite her.

'Give me your watch,' she commanded, so I took it off and gave it to her. She held it in her hand and closed her eyes. After a few moments, she opened them again. 'I feel sadness – and also resistance. I feel scepticism, but this will change.' She handed me a deck of cards. 'Think about what you'd like to ask, then shuffle the cards.'

'I . . . there's nothing I want to know specifically.'

'Just shuffle, then,' said Betty. 'The cards will reveal all.'

I did as I was told.

'Now split the cards and put them into three piles from the right.'

Again I followed her instruction.

Betty took the top cards from the middle pile and laid them out in front of her. She studied them for a while then glanced at me. 'Give me your hands,' she said. I put my hands out and she took them into hers, turned them palm up and studied them. She closed her eyes for a few moments. I felt slightly spooked. She let go of my hands and put hers over the crystal ball. Again she closed her eyes. *I wonder what baloney she's going to come out with*, I thought as I glanced around the interior of the tent. I caught my reflection in a mirror at the back. A tall, slim girl with brown eyes stared back at me. I was wearing my jeans with my favourite jacket: plum velvet with a nipped in waist and tiny buttons right up to the high neck. I got it for Christmas last year from my favourite shop, Steam Punk, and have worn it constantly ever since. I love the clothes there, they're kind of Victorian Gothic. I've asked for a pair of ankle boots from there for my birthday in June. Their Catherine Victorian boots. Black with a delicate heel, unlike the clompy ones that are in the shops at the moment. Effy says I look like Bellatrix Lestrange from the Harry Potter movies. The cheek. We just have different tastes in clothes, that's all. I like old-fashioned. Effy's style is more up-to-date.

Betty's voice brought me back from my fashion fantasy. 'Jo,' she said.

'Yes.'

'You haven't found love in this lifetime, have you?'

Effy's been filling her in, I thought as I shook my head. *I'll kill her when I get out of here.*

'No. Not exactly.' I laughed. 'But hey, I'm only seventeen!'

Betty didn't laugh, in fact she had a strange look on her face. Her eyes had glazed and, oh lord, she was starting to sway slightly. *Should I make a run for it?* I wondered as I checked behind me for the exit.

'You have travelled far through time to be here.

There is no co-incidence, it is all predestined.' Betty closed her eyes, became still and started to speak in a deeper voice. A voice that had authority. 'You have not found love, but you will.'

Me and a thousand others, I thought but I couldn't help but listen and stare. Betty was putting on a good act.

'You can find love, Jo. The reason you have not so far is because you have it imprinted in your unconscious that love is painful and that is why you have not found your soul-mate. In this lifetime, you must break the pattern.'

Whoa, I thought. *That's way heavy. She's right about me thinking love is painful but imprinted in my unconscious?* I did *not* like what I was hearing. I glanced back at the exit flap. Half of me wanted to run, part of me was intrigued. I decided to stay. I could have a good laugh about it later with Effy and Tash.

'I see a boy – you once knew him and he was your soul-mate,' Betty continued. She spoke fast, still in the same deeper voice. 'It was a great love. Powerful. He was your true love. It was in a previous life. We have all had many lives but this love was in your last life. You were a governess ... your name was Henrietta Gleeson. It was the end of the nineteenth century and you worked in a London doctor's house. This doctor had children. Two. A young boy who you were employed to care for, and an older one . . .' She lifted her head slightly to the right as if she was listening to someone. 'Howard. His name was Howard. A boy of nineteen. He was your soul-mate and yet . . .' She stopped, as though listening once again. 'Something happened to keep you apart.'

Typical, I thought. *Bad luck in this lifetime and bad luck back then too. Cool story, though. I wonder how many other people she's spun it to.*

Betty opened her eyes and looked directly at me. Right into me. 'Jo. This is important. As you are back in this lifetime, so is he. Like you, he has travelled far through time to be here. In this life, you must find him. He is your soul-mate. You were meant to be together. You *must* find him if you are ever to be happy in love.'

I felt a shiver go up my spine but I wasn't going to let her get to me. 'Was he by any chance tall, dark and handsome?'

'You may scoff at what you hear, many do. I simply tell what I see. It is always *your* choice to make of it what you will but this boy from your past, he *is* your destiny. You can believe me and try to find him or dismiss what I say and drift from one meaningless love affair to another, never finding the true contentment that your soul could know with him. You must choose.'

You're beginning to freak me out, I thought, then we both jumped as someone entered the tent behind us. It was a blonde lady in her twenties. 'Are you still doing readings?' she asked Betty.

'Have you any more questions, Jo?' Betty asked me, returning to her normal voice.

I shook my head. I felt light-headed. 'Um. No, thanks. I'm fine.' I got up and Betty beckoned the lady to take my place.

Another sucker, I thought. *I bet she even tells her the same story.*

TO BE CONTINUED ... IN *LOVE AT SECOND SIGHT*, COMING SOON!

About the Author

Cathy Hopkins lives in Bath, England with her husband and three cats, Dixie, Georgia and Otis. Cathy has been writing since 1986 and started writing teenage fiction in 2000. She spends most of her time in her writing turret pretending to write books but is actually in there listening to music, hippie dancing and checking her facebook page. So far Cathy has had fifty three books published, some of which are available in thirty three languages.

She is looking for the answers to why we're here, where we've come from and what it's all about. She is also looking for the perfect hairdresser. Apart from that, Cathy has joined the gym and spends more time than is good for her making up excuses as to why she hasn't got time to go. You can visit her on Facebook, or at www.cathyhopkins.com